Also from Skyhorse Publishing

The Zen of Zombie: Better Living Through The Undead

The Vampire Survival Guide
How to Fight, and Win, Against the Undead

Scott Bowen
Illustrations by Adam Bozarth

Skyhorse Publishing

Disclaimer: While clearly a work of humor, this book is also a work of fiction, and its author and publisher assume no liability for those readers who act upon the fictive instructions herein.

Skyhorse Publishing books may be purchased in bulk at special discounts for sales promotion, corporate gifts, fund raising, or educational purposes. Special editions can also be created to specifications. For details, contact Special Sales Department, Skyhorse Publishing, 555 Eighth Avenue, Suite 903, New York, NY 10018 or info@skyhorsepublishing.com.

www.skyhorsepublishing.com

10 9 8 7 6 5 4 3 2 1

Library of Congress Cataloging-in-Publication Data

Bowen, Scott.
 The vampire survival guide : how to fight and win against the undead / Scott Bowen ; illustrations by Adam Bozarth.
     p. cm.
 ISBN 978-1-60239-274-8 (alk. paper)
 1. Vampires—Humor. I. Title.
 PN6231.V27B69 2008
 818'.607—dc22
                                    2008012883

Printed in China

CONTENTS

Introduction

Vampire Uprisings in America

Numerous countries around the world have experienced periods of vampire epidemics or what have been quaintly referred to as "waves of vampire hysteria." Towns and small regions were suddenly lousy with the bloodsucking undead in:

- Serbia, 1730.
- East Prussia, 1750.
- Northern England, 1890.
- Canton Province, China, 1900.

Regular people found themselves in a situation unlike anything they had ever imagined, and those who were unprepared or not up to the task faced dire consequences. Many were sucked dry and left for dust, while others were transmogrified into the vampire ranks.

In America, this has happened only a few times, and the rare incidents have often been misinterpreted as localized outbreaks of disease, mass murder, or mass hysteria. Over the past two hundred years, however, a significant population of vampires has come to reside in the United States. Small cells and larger covens (united, organized groups of vampires dedicated to a particular vampire family or charismatic vampire leader) have long been careful to draw little attention and furtively take only enough blood to survive.

But much more brazen vampire behavior is on the rise.

American intelligence services and academics have described this as a kind of vampiric Manifest Destiny, with bloodsucking attacks on Americans resulting in numerous deaths, abductions, and, in a number of cases, transformation of humans into vampires.

The main factor in this development is the *irresistible blood feast* that has resulted from American's overabundant appetites. In 2008, one in every three Americans was classified as obese. In 1995, Mississippi was the only state in the union where the average body mass index (BMI) was over 25. At the time of this writing, the populations of forty-seven of the fifty states have an average body mass index of 25 or more. We're a country of slow-moving, oversized bags of blood—blood that is literally clogged with nutrients that could provide a feast of untold proportions to a race of undead humans that, despite their heightened physical and sensory powers, continually face the conundrum of finding enough blood to drink to stay alive.

Think about it this way: The Plains Indians followed the bison across the animal's natural range. Early American whalers followed whales to various oceans around the world. But when those resources ran out in a given region, the pursuers turned to other places or other game. Now, our calorie-gobbling American population presents itself as an irresistible, once-in-a-vampire-lifetime food source to an indigenous, secretive, voracious predator group:

- The *upir*.
- The *vukodlak*.
- *Nosferatu.*
- The *vampyre*.

A second significant factor is the lack of central control or authority in the world of competing vampire covens. An estimated 450,000 vampires dwell within America's borders. Competition for territory and steady food sources is apparently reaching a crescendo, a moment in American vampire history that will bring about large shifts in vampire demographics and power. In other words, vampires will need more blood as they fight over a significant but limited amount of blood, akin to human conflicts over natural resources.

So they're coming for us—they're going to be spying on us, cataloging us, preying upon us, and battling vampire-to-vampire right in the middle of our hometowns.

The initial stages of these uprisings will be reported sporadically, as small cells or covens begin hunting humans in numerous locations—urban, suburban, and rural. As before, this violence will be attributed to serial killers, gangs, drug abuse, hallucination, or errant indie filmmaking. But as newspaper stories stack up, and security and intelligence services learn more and more about what is happening, near and far, in towns with attractive populations of victims (the unsuspecting, the unarmed, the overfed) the facts will become starkly clear: *Many undead are among us.*

Americans, chubby as we are, can't take this kind of thing sitting down.

That's where this book comes in. This is your guide to defending yourself and your family and fighting back. *Vampires can be stopped*—with massive amounts of carefully directed violence. There's really no other way. You're not going to get them on *Dr. Phil* and talk them out of it (though it would be pretty enjoyable to watch them drain that rotund blowhard dry). You're going to have to stockpile supplies, stay up late, psych yourself up to unknown levels of confidence, and blow large holes in a variety of undead beings that will be traipsing, sneaking, and slithering around your neighborhood and possibly into your house.

Get your game face on now. This isn't going to be your favorite episode of *Buffy the Vampire Slayer* or your usual Friday night playing *Vampire: The Masquerade*. Forget that.

You're fighting for your life.

Chapter 1

The Nature of the Beast

Many Americans will take little interest in vampires beyond wanting to know how many might be lurking about and how much ammunition is in the cupboard. But knowing your enemy isn't a bad idea, especially when you're up against one so strange. Vampires don't have many exploitable weaknesses, but they do have traits that might play into defensive strategies.

A Quick Guide to Vampires and the Vampire Uprising

- Vampires can feed on any kind of blood but derive greatest pleasure and nutrition from human blood.
- Vampires cannot turn into fluids or gases, or wolves, bats, or any other animals. They are not shape shifters. They cannot fly. They cannot travel through time. They are not minions of Satan, as they are no more certain the devil exists than we humans are.
- Vampires do not live forever, in the sense of to the end of the earth, but they can live for several millennia. Few, however, actually do.
- Vampires can function during the daytime but will suffer skin burns in direct sun and will die if trapped in sunlight for hours.
- Vampires come in all human shapes and sizes, skills, interests, and intelligences.
- Vampirism is caused by a virus that becomes active through its chemical interaction with vampire hemo-

globin. A vampire must first infect its victim with the virus and then feed its own blood to the victim to initiate transformation into a vampire.

- The vampire virus is terrifically primitive, harkening back to some partially animal state of human development (this accounts for the often infernal explanation of the origin of vampires). Thus, vampires possess animal-like strengths and skills: They are extremely quick, quiet, and stealthy.
- Vampires can survive on small amounts oxygen for extended periods and can slow their heart rates dramatically, enabling them to rest without feeding for significant periods when blood is scarce.
- The vampire's senses of hearing, smell, and taste are acute, allowing them to know when humans are near through heat signatures, slight vibrations, and scent. They feel pain but are troubled by only the worst injuries or disorders.

The Underlying Cause

Various literary, religious, and folkloric traditions trace the origins of vampirism to demigods, demons, or demonic possession. Other traditions trace the origin of vampires to the difficulties and pains of childbirth. But numerous modern-day considerations of evidence gathered over centuries suggests some kind of systemic physiological disorder caused by a gene-altering virus. The susceptibility to this disease seems to be inherent in humankind, as vampirism is a phenomenon in many cultures around the world. Most likely, the virus responsible for vampirism evolved along with humans.

Vampirism and Disease

No one has ever pinpointed the location of the first case of vampirism, which would be akin to pinpointing the first case of smallpox. As recently as the 1960s, researchers suggested the collective of metabolic diseases called porphyria may

Random Question: Can vampires turn my dog into a vampire dog? (Because I think that would be really cool.)

Sorry to thwart your diabolical plot to create an army of vampire dogs, but the answer is no. Most mammalian animals, especially dogs, universally sense and avoid vampires. Unlike rabies, which affects both animals and humans, the vampire virus affects only humans in terms of creating a vampire, though certain other mammals might carry the virus, including dogs, cats, and livestock, and could possibly transfer it to humans (no one knows for sure how readily this can happen). But an animal bitten by a vampire that is also made to consume vampire blood won't turn into a vampire—the animal genetics are simply not right for this. And this will not create a were-dog, were-cat, or were-cow. Lycanthropy has wholly different causes and origins.

Your dog, in fact, might turn out to be truly your best friend during these crazy times, as his excellent senses will warn of approaching bloodsuckers. *Do what he says.*

explain vampirism, though this has since been debunked. A trait of extreme porphyria—sensitivity to light—and the highly speculative notion that sufferers of the disease would drink blood to fight the symptoms (porphyria can be treated with injections of heme) suggest some parallels to vampirism, though hardly in any sufficient way to make it synonymous with the attributes of vampires. During various periods in Europe, tuberculosis and the plague were thought to cause vampire symptoms. But neither of these proved true, although vampires have done their best to exploit the camouflage of an epidemic. (Friedrich Murnau, the German director of *Nosferatu, Eine Symphonie des Grauens*, transplanted the Dracula story to Bremen in 1838 to coincide with a historical outbreak of the plague in the city.)

Transfer of the Vampire Virus

The vampire virus enters people the same ways that rabies or hepatitis is transmitted: through direct fluid-to-fluid contact via bites, open wounds, sex, and if someone sneezes on his hand and then shakes your hand and then you put your fingers in your mouth. This *does not* turn a person into a vam-

pire, but it is a precursor to potential transformation. Actual transformation occurs only when a victim ingests a large dose of vampire blood. A vampire who intends to turn a victim into a vampire feeds that person blood directly from his veins. Some vampires that want to carefully cultivate victims as a food source, without infecting or converting them, will drink from a sharp tube mounted on a spout that is poked into the victim's neck, thus having no direct contact with the wound. *Millions of people carry the vampire virus*, but it remains dormant until united with a significant amount of vampire hemoglobin. Then you're on your way, Elvira.

Mutations of Vampirism

Because vampirism appears to be caused by disease, and given that vampires are former human beings, the vampire virus seems to do two things: One: It mutates over time. Two: It can affect each new vampire in different ways, from the very subtle to the grotesque.

You may encounter vampires from many years—even centuries—ago, who were originally infected with an older strain that hasn't changed. In similarly old vampires, the virus may have mutated, altering both the vampire and the humans it transforms in novel ways. For this reason, you may confront vampires that appear mostly human and some that seem more like ghouls, beasts, or monsters.

It's going to be a real *carnival* out there.

One particular note: Vampires can be identified by their DNA, but it won't match the DNA of the person from whom the vampire arose. Thus, trying to ID someone who was turned into a vampire by testing vampire blood won't work. However, you can ID a vampire whose DNA has already been recorded. Vampires have one blood type, labeled O-V. They are universal donors and recipients among themselves.

Vampire Physiology and Needs

The vampire is a beast designed for survival, because it can live on two things found everywhere: oxygen and blood. You don't see very many overweight vampires, either, because their metabolisms shed fat. Sure, some have refrigerators full of blood and sit around playing Wii all night (they're good at golf), but very few are sedentary. Their physiological disposition—overwhelming hunger, verging on the desperation of starvation—compels them to hunt.

Vampire Fact:
The folkloric anti-vampire defenses of European cultures include the use of poppy seeds, mustard seeds, millet, and other seeds. Because vampires were thought to have compulsive tendencies, villagers scattered the seeds around a suspected vampire's grave or home in the belief that a vampire would be compelled to stop to count or collect the seeds, delaying itself so long that the sun will drive it back to its lair.

Solar Sensitivity

Vampires can move about during the day, and they can tolerate direct sunlight for very brief periods of time, say a minute or two, before their skin begins to burn. Vampires can cover themselves—usually in white and silver over a layer of black—and wear goggles to simultaneously reflect and protect themselves from the sun. But this is only a temporary fix, as ultraviolet rays will eventually penetrate the layers after a short time, perhaps an hour, and begin to cause internal damage. This trait is simply part of the nature of vampirism, similar to human sensitivity to the sun, only much more pronounced. In the vampire's case, solar sensitivity is probably the result of deep cellular changes that affect melanin production. A vampire will become severely burned and ultimately will die if left in the sun, but in some cases a sunburned vampire can be reanimated.

Vampire Bodily Systems

The former human's circulatory system is the vampire's digestive system. Ingested blood passes through the stomach wall directly into the bloodstream. The vampire heart beats much more slowly than the human heart, simply to keep up a minimum blood pressure, while the bodily tissues—mostly muscle and skeletal tissues and the kidneys—are literally bathed in blood after ingestion. Due to a certain level of cellular breakdown, the stomach and intestines atrophy greatly. The liver, spleen, and pancreas remain active only

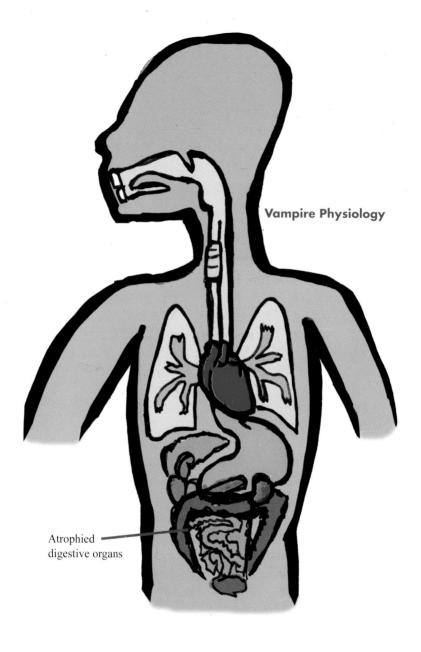

Vampire Physiology

Atrophied
digestive organs

to the degree to which they play a role in creating new blood tissue. A vampire's powerful lungs oxygenate blood quickly and completely. This capability of fully bathing muscle tissue in highly oxygenated blood lends the bloodsuckers heightened strength and speed (imagine blood doping times ten), although it is something even more animal in their nature—something as yet unknown—that allows them their supreme athleticism.

The Thirst for Blood

Vampires who, in their human lives, were drug addicts—even heroin addicts—have described to researchers and interrogators a need for blood that is much stronger than any craving for a drug (all major state security agencies—the Mossad, Bundespolizei, old KGB, MI5, and CIA—have captured and interrogated vampires in top-secret programs). While vampires are capable of high levels of self-control in the search for blood, they often find their hunger and desire to seek blood irresistible. This arises out of what is thought to be a primitive effect of the vampire virus: Vampires devolve to some kind of prehuman physiological form that had the ability to survive on just one very basic and widely found food substance. At some point this must have been an evolutionary advantage for some prehumans. But as *Homo sapiens* evolved in various regions, both slowly and quickly, omnivorousness arose, along with religious or spiritual taboos about cannibalism.

Suspended States

Vampires can suffer exsanguination (complete loss of blood) due to major physical injury or the severing of an artery. Younger vampires might expire under such circumstances, but established, older vampires will fall into a state of suspended cellular activity and can lie dormant for many days or years. They can later be revived with mass transfusions of vampire blood. This does not always work, and recovery can take weeks. But covens are able to maintain continuity of leadership and intelligence by doing so.

Life Expectancy

A vampire can easily live for hundreds of years—perhaps a few millennia—with a lot of stealth, care, efficiency, and intelligence. They are not, however, immortal in the sense that they can live forever. Flesh eventually fails.

Vampire Likes and Dislikes

Vampires might be highly sentient and opinionated, but they are also at the mercy of their bodies and have universal traits in terms of how they deal with their physical environment. *All animals have limits.*

Vampires like . . .

Effective cultivation of blood sources: Vampires admire other vampires that seize and hold a large territory of quality prey. They also admire bloodsuckers that, when faced with limited but viable blood sources, are able to feed on them for significant periods of time without arousing suspicions or fears, something that calls for highly practiced skills of hypnotism or seduction.

Deadly animals: While vampires cannot shape-shift into animals, they do have a great admiration for cats, bears, bulls, spiders, hornets, scorpions, eagles, snakes, and sharks. Most wild and domestic mammals quickly sense, fear, and flee vampires, so most creatures that vampires keep as pets are reptiles, amphibians, fish, and insects. Occasionally, various felines hand-raised by vampires tolerate them.

Airplanes: Certain high-ranking vampires do own and make use of private aircraft, but very carefully, given the significant bureaucratic regulation of airplanes. But many vampires admire the great usefulness of aircraft and covet them.

Vampires dislike . . .

Water: Vampires avoid immersion if possible, as the effect of evaporation on their skin lowers their body temperatures to the point that it affects both their digestion and enjoyment of digesting blood. This pleasure is too valued to risk.

Fire: Combustion is symbolic of death for every vampire and is rarely used as an implement in usual hunting and feeding activities. In coven-on-coven wars, vampires have been known to set fire to a competing coven's house or castle to destroy the structure and any vampire bodies inside, but this is not a frequent event. Vampires know full well how easily fire can get out of control and how impractical it is for small tactical issues.

Modern weapons: You most likely won't see vampires using firearms or anything more powerful, as they are both enamored with and largely controlled by their animal-like instincts and physical abilities. They prefer to hunt and feed using sheer skill and a few scant implements (daggers, si-

Random Question: If I wear garlands of garlic, will that keep vampires away from me?

For centuries, garlic has played a major role in folk medicine. Its health benefits are undisputed. But as a repellent of vampires, it is ineffective. In much the same way that a citronella candle is distasteful to mosquitoes, some vampires simply don't like the odor of garlic (it smells slightly similar to moldered, dead vampire flesh, and thus discomfortingly suggests the physical corruption of the vampire itself). But if you've ever been attacked by some of those hard-core Florida or Alaska mosquitoes, you know that citronella has real limits. Garlic is the same when it comes to vampires. Sure, give it a try—have a bunch on hand.

But don't expect the leeches to run away if you toss some garlic powder in the air.

You'll do better tossing grenades.

phons, glass cutters). Only when covens find themselves under massive attack—by humans or other covens—do they resort to using firearms that they have stockpiled. They also prefer to elude human gunfire than return fire.

Vampires that help humans: Vampires that forswear human blood and attempt to help humans fight against predatory bloodsuckers are rare, but they do exist. Predatory vampires view this as high treason and will dedicate themselves to finding and destroying turncoat vampires.

Canines: Owing to some epic contest between early primates and prehistoric canines, the virus imprints an intense hatred of dogs on the vampire. Remember, this is a gene-altering illness, possessing its own DNA, and it rewires the victim's brain with very old instincts.

Sizes, Shapes, and Abilities

A later chapter will discuss various home and apartment fortifications to keep vampires out when local or regional uprisings are particularly intense. But as noted in the earlier rundown of vampire abilities, they are not supernaturally capable, just immensely strong for their size. If you've ever had the displeasure of being attacked by a young cougar or a large monkey, you will understand how wild things that don't seem to have much bulk can inflict serious damage very quickly.

From Dwarfs to Giants

Vampires traditionally are highly selective about whom they transform into a vampire. Most often, they transform people they wish to have in their coven, or who they think would make powerful vampire allies. Some also do so for companionship and matrimony. But vampires also tend to convert people who are much like themselves. So while you might encounter pairs or covens of vampires of highly similar physique and nature, you will also encounter the occasional group of little-person vampires or seven-foot-tall, 300-pound vampires. There are also elderly vampires and child vampires, which will all attack you with alacrity; you won't have much choice but to stop them, regardless of how creepy it is to knock off grandmothers and second-graders.

Vampires, however, lead rather rough physical lives, and you will find that even those leeches that seem quite elegant or handsome will bear numerous marks, scars, and bent or

Vampire Fact:

One of the most intriguing shape-shifting vampire-like creatures is the *loogaroo* of Haitian folklore. A *loogaroo* collects warm human blood at night so that she (usually *loogaroos* are old women) can deliver it to Satan in exchange for magical powers. To reach a victim, the *loogaroo* removes her skin and takes the form of a flickering ball of light that can enter any home. This Haitian name is a mistaken adaptation of the French term for werewolf: *loup-garou*.

reattached parts. Although rarely without physical defect, superior bloodsuckers will seem most human in appearance, albeit with skin color, eyes, and faces that can appear downright alien. Lesser vampires will be visibly defective: hunchbacked, missing limbs, psychotic, or disfigured by disease from their former human lives.

Altered Physical Appearance

The vampire virus causes some limited skeletal changes. Bones become denser and stronger, as red bone marrow in major bones is a source of red blood cells. In some cases the skeleton becomes a bit enlarged, causing some bone surfaces to be more prominent. Shoulders, collarbones, elbows, wrists, knuckles, hips, and knees can all seem just slightly bigger than that of a human. The skull can also slightly enlarge, just enough to be noticeable, with cheekbones, chins, and eye sockets a bit more defined in some vampires.

Strength, Senses, and Intelligence

Vampires are warm-blooded, otherwise they would have none of the strength and abilities they possess, but they contain their body heat more efficiently than humans. Although they can occasionally be located using thermal imaging, they do not leave very clear thermal trails.

How strong is a vampire? In general, any given vampire possesses twice the strength of a terrifically athletic human of the same size. You're not going to win a hand-to-hand fight with a vampire, so forget what they're telling you at your dojo; Bruce Lee would have his hands full with any vampire (although in *Game of Death* he did beat Hakim, played by Kareem Abdul-Jabbar, a character who was sensitive to light).

How fast is a vampire? They're capable of very fast, short sprints. Consider that vampires in times of starvation easily caught deer, horses, and dogs, and you'll have an idea of their speed across a short distance. Vampires can also cover a lot of ground in one night, as a fast march is nothing to them.

Vampire sight is adapted to a nocturnal life but tends to be most effective over short distances, up to fifty feet. Daylight is bothersome to their eyes, and a direct beam of a powerful spotlight dazzles them momentarily.

Vampires also seem to possess a kind of clairvoyant ability to detect humans. Part of this arises from their acute sense of

Vampire Fact:

Slavs and Gypsies had very definite views of vampires as highly sexual beings. Male vampires were thought to have a sex drive strong enough to raise them from the grave and return them to their widows. Dead men suspected of being vampires were sometimes reported to have erections when uncovered in their graves. In Russian folklore, vampires often possessed strong sexual traits, appearing as attractive strangers intent on seducing young women.

smell and taste. Vampire noses and tongues are sensitive to heat sources, much like a snake's, helping them locate prey in the dark. But vampires also have highly tuned skin surfaces that act similarly to a lateral line on a fish or a snake's belly: They can feel vibrations in the air, even those caused by extreme human emotions. Thus, *vampires can sense and smell human fear.* (You can't mask fear, though some products, such as "Murder Musk" and "Fear Screen," have come on the market and purport to cover the odor of adrenaline and other pheromones released during periods of intense emotion. They don't seem to work.)

Random Question: Is it true that a vampire can go all night?

Well, yeah, they're nocturnal.

More specifically: Vampires do have sex, but sex itself cannot compete with their bloodlust. Blood is life, as the saying goes. Think of the best meal you ever had, and now imagine if that meal made you really, really high—that's what drinking blood is like for a vampire. Everything in a vamp's life revolves around getting and consuming blood. Vampires might have sex with one another, but as a corollary pleasure to feeding. They also will have sex with victims as part of the ritual of drinking blood, or as part of the transformation ritual.

People who have survived sex with a vampire usually confess to a pretty rough night. Vampires can achieve orgasm but often require much more vigorous engagement than people do. If you find a house full of broken furniture every morning, you're probably dating a vampire. And that's no hickey, either.

As far as intelligence goes, a vampire starts out as smart as the person from which it was made and then improves from there, assuming the person from which it came was not brain-damaged or deranged, which has happened. (You ain't seen nothing until you see a paranoid-schizophrenic vampire.) Vampires develop tactically brilliant minds out of necessity. They are frequently masters of chess, and vampires that have been interrogated by American intelligence officers have demonstrated terrifically high levels of intellect and a mental ruggedness that makes them greatly impervious to the mind tricks used during interrogations. Vampires have incredibly good memory skills; some have near-photographic memories. Much of this results from a kind of mind-stamping psyche that, again, harkens back to primitive necessity and evolutionary adaptation.

Vampires are also notoriously seductive. How else can you lure someone toting a gun close enough to you to bite without that person taking a shot? This ability emanates from the vampire's power of giving an "immortal" existence to a human victim: The vampiric gaze suspends you in your fear of dying that very moment and then seduces you through your hope that the vampire won't kill you; thus, by surrendering you free yourself from the fear. *Twisted, ain't it?*

Drinking Blood

Vampires develop fangs that grow in place of the normal canines, which either shift back or get pushed down and out. The fangs are long and sharp enough to penetrate to draw blood from blood vessels. But vampires, like people, are not always satisfied with their natural traits and seek to surpass them. Some vampires use special-made stilettos and daggers to draw blood from deeper veins or arteries. Others use stainless-steel flutes that have a sharpened tube at one end that they insert into a vein or artery, especially the carotid artery if a large, quick feed is needed, and the life of the victim is of no concern.

Appearance, Dress, and Personal Style

Vampires inhabit their own world but often with many of the trappings of contemporary human life. Many prefer life in houses to life on the road. They tend to their appearances. Many will retain some of the vestments of the era in which they were transformed (1800s, 1950s, 1985), or some item of fashion to indicate their origins while adapting their appearance as they age.

Skin and Eye Color

Regardless of the victim's race—Asian, African, Caucasian, Pacific, and so forth—changes of the skin occur with the transformation to vampire. In general, vampire skin becomes paler than the skin color prior to transformation, but other changes can occur as well: Olive-skinned victims can take on a paler, reddish-tinged shade as vampires. White-skinned victims-cum-vampires can become a hazy gray or porcelain blue. Black- and brown-skinned victims can become bluish or tawny. All vampires also suffer skin discolorations such as varicosities and bruises.

Vampires almost always have eyes that are bloodshot or blood-stained in the sclera; their irises darken in color and become nearly opaque, making the pupils barely visible. Such eye traits are a key identifier of the vampire.

Facial Features

Many vampires can take on a slightly lupine or vulpine face due to changes in the skull structure. Lips can range from brownish red to red. The fangs usually do not protrude. Many vampires use makeup to cover facial skin discolorations or to alter their general hue.

Numerous vampires will have severely altered or disfigured facial features, owing to the chaotic and violent circumstances under which they became vampires. These undead will appear to have just a skull with a thin skin stretched across it and deep-set eyes in black sockets (the result of having nearly died as a mortal before being transformed, as seen in victims of plagues); others will have ghoulish countenances, with missing noses or eyes or even skull plates (these frequently being the wounded of war who were turned into vampires while lying on the battlefield or in a field hospital). Again, the essential identifying feature is the eyes, which are unmistakable.

Human Head   **Vampire Head**

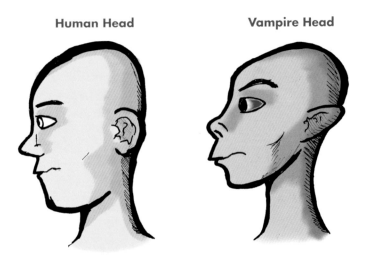

Fashionable, Yet Practical

Most people get their sense of how vampires dress from movies and video games. The bloodsuckers are either all gussied up for a night at the opera or sporting some kind of body armor/bondage wear. A few others dress like rejects from 1980s heavy-metal bands.

Many vampires do insist on a level of fashion. They have reputations among themselves to maintain. This is balanced by the necessities of hunting for blood. Vampires on the prowl most often wear dark clothing that makes little noise. It must allow for movement and present few surfaces that could get snagged on branches or windowsills, and so they often wear wool or silk. Only very soft leathers are quiet. Motorcycle jackets tend to make noise, as do latex and significant body armor. Vampires do sometimes wear a very tightly woven chain mail that can form a smooth, quiet layer under their clothing. This can ward against shotgun blasts at a significant distance; up close it is not effective. Many vampires also have taken to wearing the newest, thin, quiet American military clothing made for special reconnaissance units.

Behind the closed doors of their coven hideouts, vampires wear all varieties of fashion—everything from Tudor finery to Yves Saint Laurent to your basic gray hoodie and Carhartt cargo pants. A lot of their fashion choices depend upon the era from which they came, but vampires from a time of complicated clothing (say, the vests and coats of Revolutionary America) or a life of insufficient clothing (beggar's rags) often come to enjoy most modern materials and styles of clothing.

Daggers, Cars, and Jewelry

As said, vampires might take up arms to defend a coven's location, but otherwise venture forth without much more than stilettos. But these blades are often very well made and highly appointed with jewels and valuable metals. Frequently, the style and engraving of a dagger will identify a vampire as belonging to specific coven. You might want to pick one of these up as a souvenir, but if you do, don't go sporting it on your hunting belt until after the uprising is stopped, because if a vampire finds that you've killed one of its kind, your chances of simply being fed upon and left half dead will disappear in a painful session of disembowelment and mayhem.

As for transportation, vampires have a weakness for luxury cars. No one is sure why. Perhaps it's partly to camouflage themselves as well-to-do Europeans, Russians, or Americans on their way to a late dinner. It may also arise from a desire to travel in style given a vampire's background of having to sneak, skulk, and creep to find its food. Whatever the case, be wary of nighttime travelers driving Mercedes-Benz CLKs, Jaguar XJ7s, BMW M3s, Audi R8s, Aston Martin Rapides, and Maseratis. Groups of vampires have sometimes been seen in late-model Land Rovers.

Vampire Fact:

Occultists who have focused on myths that portray vampires not as physical entities but as paranormal forces—ghosts or demons—theorize that the astral body (a second, invisible human body that separates from the physical body at death) could act as a vampire. When a person drifts into a coma or some other deep state mistaken for death and is buried prematurely, the astral body separates and moves among the living, sucking their blood and thus passing the nourishment to the main body, keeping it alive. Other occultists have viewed vampirism as a remnant of human force or intelligence that lingers after death and can briefly take nourishment from the living, sapping their life force, before disintegrating itself.

Vampires also have a predilection for various kinds of high-end jewelry. Those that in their previous human lives wore a lot of jewelry often carry this over into their vampire lives. As a group, they tend to favor big, colored stones—rubies, sapphires, and emeralds—and silver instead of gold. There are many vampire jewelry makers that create pieces unique to covens and individual vampires. Frequently, covens have a specific stone worn by members. Again, be careful what you snatch off vampires that you've killed, because wearing such baubles can be risky. Your best bet is to sell vampire jewelry in the black market (discussed in chapter 4).

Vulnerabilities

Despite the mental and physical abilities of vampires, they do have their weak spots. Remember, the vampire is based on a human frame, and many of the odd natures or bad habits of people come through and are amplified in vampires. You can exploit these with various lures, deceits, and traps.

Extreme Curiosity

If you observe a vampire entering a new structure, you will find something terrier-like about its behavior (believing itself unseen). The vampire will observe very intently every surface and every object, as it is a vampire's habit to quickly familiarize itself with new surroundings. An older blood-sucker will have seen a great deal in its lifetime and will

Random Question: Will blaring classical music scare away vampires like it scares away the skater kids at the strip mall?

First, skateboarding is not a crime. Second, no.

Experiments in anti-vampire weaponry have never yielded any sort of sound wave or electric impulse that affects them. Many vampires enjoy classical music, and, once your loud music alerts them to your presence in the house, they will have a truly wonderful time sucking you dry to *The Rite of Spring*; or, if you want them to think you're really hip, *Einstein on the Beach* (but do you really want to die to a Philip Glass soundtrack?).

not be impressed with much; it will, nonetheless, be greatly curious about a device, mechanism, or artwork it has never seen before.

While setting traps for vampires isn't easy (see chapter 4), you can place a unique or unusual object in a location that will allow you to observe the vampire for a moment and, indeed, have a clear shot at it while it inspects the thing it has found.

Great Egotism

The undead put great stock in their skills, intellect, and adversarial role against humankind. Leaders of covens and elder, more powerful vampires often have outsized views of

Random Question: Do covens ever admit human members, even on a provisional basis?

No, never, not even covens with members that have attempted to cooperate with humans. Few victims have ever survived seeing the inside of a coven's headquarters. Most victims taken to a coven's lair are killed due to excessive feeding or kept for a brief time as a slave before being drained to death; very few are transformed into vampires. Vampire covens are among the most secretive organizations in the world.

themselves. This puts them at increased vulnerability to insult, and negative criticism will often draw a vampire to its critic. While this should not be undertaken idly, experienced vampire-killer teams can summon specific vampires or a select few vampires by mailing letters, sending text messages, or scribbling graffiti that delivers poisonous words, such as: "The vampire Hercule of the Pittsburgh coven is a bastard of low birth who can't stop drinking pig blood"; or, "The vampires who came to 704 Hauser Street last night ran shrieking like girls when they heard us load our shotguns."

Of course, once you ask for it, you're going to get it.

Gluttony to Distraction

At times, vampires will gorge themselves on blood, emulating the binge eating that afflicts their American prey. They can literally fill themselves with blood until they cannot contain anymore and their bodies go *squish* and they leak blood profusely. Blood feasts often turn out this way: messy, messy, messy. They can happen when a group of hungry vampires finds a large number of easy victims or discovers a store of blood hidden by a coven. But unlike an American in a food coma, a blood-saturated vampire is running on rocket fuel and enters a highly active, even agitated, state. This trait isn't easy to turn to the human defender's advantage, as such blood binging usually takes place behind closed doors. Some people, however, have set up vampire traps using large amounts of livestock blood, as a barrel or big trough full of cattle blood can induce very hungry or inexperienced vampires to gorge themselves.

A Note About Covens

Covens range from small, closely knit vampire cliques to large, loosely formed groups to very formal, hierarchical, secretive organizations. These collectives are part gang and part fraternal lodge; when a coven's vampires act as a group, they usually do so in an action against another coven. Vampires see little reason to unite in such force against humans; having to do so would be self-insulting, as if single vampires or duos or trios couldn't handle most humans. But covens engaged by American military or security elements will respond *in force.*

The actual names of covens are not known, or, if they are known to Western intelligence services, are most likely false. Much about covens, including what name members use to refer to the collective, is secret and codified. One known fact about covens is that they are often formed by vampires who were once part of the same human family, often to fight back against those who took their human lives.

Chapter 2

Combating Infection in Yourself and Others

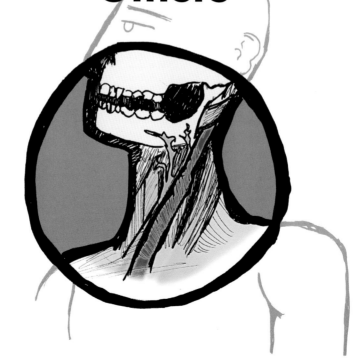

An essential part of surviving the vampire uprising is the ability to recognize vampiric traits in people who have been transformed by an attacking vampire, but who have not yet begun to take on the full physical attributes of vampirism. This chapter will show you what to look for and how to deal with a friend or family member who is transforming into vampire.

The stresses of enduring a vampire uprising, especially those lengthy periods when nightly vigils must be maintained, will wear our nerves thin. People will have outbursts. Others will retreat into themselves and become disaffected. Some people will *snap.* No amount of afternoon-TV pop psychology will begin to help Americans cope.

Amid all these neuroses will be people transforming into vampires. Their apparent personality disorders will blossom into visibly dangerous traits. The actual physiological transformation, once identified, can be subdued and possibly stopped with various medical treatments if administered early enough—when the victim appears to come out of a coma-like sleep that is seemingly attributable to blood loss but is, in fact, a deep neurological state of early transformation. Once a victim begins to exhibit the physical and personality traits described below, however, the chances of slowing or halting the transformation are slim.

Victims will have no ability to resist the extreme conversion going on inside themselves. Highly socialized, trusting, and community-centered people will often clearly state that they are suffering something unknown to themselves (their memories of being bled, and then fed vampire blood held deeply in their subconscious) and will engage with people attempting to treat them. Those who are in a state of great physical or emotional disconnect, anger, and fear at the time of their infection, however, will find that their psychological state creates a barrier between them and their would-be rescuers.

Note: Much of the survival tactics in this guide hinge on your being a member of a family group or a team of friends, although there will be those instances in which you are alone. So through this text there will be references to "shooter teams" or "hunter teams" that will be explained fully in chapter 4, these defensive and offensive teams being assembled from your family and friends.

Changes in the Victim's Personality and Habits

While many victims who go through complete transformation will do so in the company of vampires, within the walls of vampire-claimed houses or in a coven's den, a significant number of victims will remain within their family group, and can thus be observed by other members. Once just a few signs of vampirism show, *action must be taken quickly.*

Focus and Temperament

As vampirism becomes manifest in the victim, the person will swing from a seemingly sleepwalking state to determined, intense interest in other people or ideas. His disposition will range from docile, even timid, to brash and frenetic. This back-and-forth cycle is key. Someone who has lost a lot of blood due to injury will go through a long, tiring recovery marked by little energy. This will not be spiked with sudden, energetic outbursts or sudden attractions.

Shifting from Day to Night Consciousness

As the active vampire virus continues to alter the victim, the victim will begin to show an inclination for hiding and sleeping in very dark places during the day and being completely, almost wildly, awake throughout the night. At first, witnesses may believe this is due to abuse of stimulant drugs, such as crystal meth or cocaine. But continued observation of the victim should eliminate drug abuse as a possible cause.

Really, at this point, given the fact that the family or team must suspect that this person was in the grip of a vampire, there's little other explanation for these traits. *Denial* is not a problem for the victim, but it is an extremely dangerous problem for friends and family members who just don't want to believe that good ol' Steve, or pretty little Delilah, or our faithful reference librarian Ms. Magillicutty is turning into a vampire. **Time to get real, folks.**

Loss of Appetite

This transformational trait will be nearly continuous, from the time the victim regains consciousness until you're holding her down and giving her anticonvulsive drugs. People who suffer great blood loss due to trauma do not wake up wanting Taco Bell—their system isn't giving them that message. People who suffer great blood loss and wake up in the grip of vampirism don't feel like eating much, either. Even after the victim is up and walking and chattering and flitting about in an unnerving manner, he won't sit down when you ask him to have some homemade granola.

A key sign here, however, is a lack of want for water. Injured people often wake up very thirsty, as blood loss causes severe dehydration. Sufferers of vampirism will not seek water upon waking, and if you make them drink it, they will likely cough up most of it. *Vampires hydrate with the red stuff.* So if someone who should be asking for water by the gallon actually doesn't, take keen note. (Note the rabies corollary, as this disease was once called "hydrophobia," because the victim with late-stage symptoms cannot take water at all.)

Unexplained Lustful Actions

Lust is actually pretty easily explained in humans. We want what and whom we want (usually someone we can't have).

Vampiric lust is not entirely about who the lust object is, but what the lust object *contains*.

As a part of the manic behaviors of early stage vampirism, the victim will physically press themselves upon other members of the family or team. This will seem to be for want of a kiss or embrace, or something more sexual, but the victim will do this in a baffled, clumsy way, sniffing and kissing the other person randomly, almost without affection. The rising vampire can smell the blood inside his or her object of desire but does not yet have a complete appetite for or understanding of how to get it. But they know it's there.

Vampire Fact:

A well-known, documented vampire report in Scotland is that of the vampire of Melrose Abbey, in the twelfth century. A priest, dying after a life of thoroughly unpriestly behavior, was buried on the abbey's grounds. After he appeared several times at the bed of a woman to whom the priest had served as chaplain, the woman, unbitten, complained to the monks at the abbey. Four monks set up watch on the cemetery, and one of them saw the vampire priest emerge from his grave. As the vampire approached, the monk struck him with an ax and drove the bloodsucker back into his grave. The next morning the team of monks exhumed the priest, finding his coffin full of blood and the mark of the monk's ax on his body, prompting them to cremate the body and scatter the ashes. The woman never complained of visits again.

Changes in Appearance

When a victim's physical appearance begins to change, the rising vampire in that person cannot be stopped by any medication—the rough and ready drug treatments described later in this chapter are of little use. These outward physical changes reflect extensive inner ones and signal the final phase of transformation. The metamorphosis will not be complete until the new vampire has fed several times. But by the time you see the features discussed below, you are in serious danger.

Skin Discolorations

The pallid or greatly lightened skin of the early stage of victimization might take on a slightly green or amber tinge, and surface veins will stand out in a strong bluish shade. Small varicosities will sometimes rise around joints and on

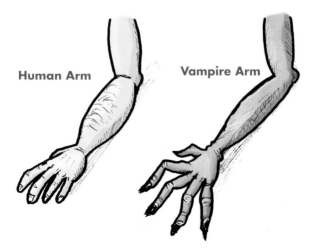

Human Arm   **Vampire Arm**

the ears and nose. This pale appearance will persist until the new vampire feeds for the first time. Fresh blood will then color the vampire's skin and might put a tinge of pink in its eyes. The skin around the eyes will darken. A vampire's physical appearance will continue to change throughout its first year.

Weight Loss and Heightened Facial Features

After going so long without food and having limited nutrients in its bloodstream, the rising vampire will appear significantly thinner than the human from which it arose, depending upon the size of the human victim. Additionally, some mild facial changes will occur, as some weight is lost from the face, and eyebrows, cheekbones, noses, and chins protrude. Skeletal changes will come along as the vampire feeds. The ironic thing about many of the vampiric transformations that will occur during the uprising is that the abundant girth of the many American victims will produce a generation of the most fleshed-out, overweight vampires ever seen in history. These pizza-gut bloodsuckers will make the excruciating thinness of a Graf Orlok seem truly a thing of a far-distant, plague-ridden past. Slowly, however, even brand-new size XXL American vampires will lose excess flesh.

Clouded or Oddly Colored Eyes

The retinal vein occlusion seen in many vampires does not appear until successive feedings and fades if a vampire is

Typical American Vampire

Graf Orlok

starving. In developing vampires, the irises can take on a slightly clouded, cataract-like sheen, while in other cases the blue, green, or brown of the victim's eyes will partially darken or grow mottled and nonuniform in coloration. This is usually seen at the final stages of the transformation, and looking into such changed eyes is a dangerous proposition: A rising vampire might begin to sense its own hypnotic powers owing to the odd attraction its new eyes will have for humans trying to determine just what is going on, and it could very well exploit this effect to lure its first victim.

Random Question: I know I'm not a vampire (I'm vegan, actually), but my paranoid friends think that I'm turning into one. How do I prove to them I'm not?

What, exactly, is causing their paranoia? Too much PCP? That might be the problem. But if they're just suffering garden-variety, everyone-different-is-dangerous paranoia, you do have a few remedies.

A stroll in bright sunlight is usually the first move. Your friends might ask you to do this several times over a few days. Indulge them; tell them to keep a calendar of how many days they think have passed since you supposedly began the transformation. After twenty days, if you're still playing beach volleyball, it's time they shut up.

Second, eat something in front of them. Vampires cannot digest actual food (meat, fruit, and so on), so scarf down a tofu burger with all the fixin's or some whole-grain veggie pizza. If you really want to make your case, report to your friends the confirmation of complete digestion (they asked for it); vampires don't do that, either.

Lastly, tell them to pick the day they think your transformation should be complete, and then make a one-hundred-dollar bet with them that you can go five days from that point without drinking blood, which would kill a new vampire. Of course, you'll have to hang out with them the whole time to prove you're right, and you'd better be careful about that paranoia, because, angel dust or not, it's a powerful mental state, and paranoid people do impulsive things, like . . . kill their friends.

Caring for the Afflicted

You need to consider and prepare for the possibility that you or someone in your family might get bitten. A vampire's bite is not the worst thing that can happen (painful death takes that award), but it's no fun. If you have no way of fighting back, a vampire will take you into an iron grasp, hold you down, and feed off you. You will be immobilized because of blood loss. The vampire might then leave you or keep you for later feeding. During that time of captivity, the vampire will use its powers of seduction and domination to make you into a (nearly) willing victim.

Keep in mind that dealing with the vampire virus is like dealing with any other virus: It can be resisted, battled, and stabilized. In and of itself, it is not the most dangerous thing. Infection with vampire blood is the bigger problem.

Cleaning the Bite Mark

If a vampire bites a victim, the mark will usually be obvious: two small, bleeding puncture wounds on the neck, arm, or possibly the leg. A victim might have multiple bite marks if attacked several times or by more than one vampire. Bacteria or other pathogens (of a non-vampiric nature) in the vampire's mouth can infect the bite mark itself.

Clean the bite holes and surrounding area with strong soap and warm water, and then disinfect with iodine. Leave the bite uncovered so that the blood can coagulate and scab over. Watch for draining pus or notable swelling. Once the bite holes have scabbed, cover them with gauze and wrap them loosely but tight enough to protect them. Watch the victim for fever or other signs of infection, such as weakness, cold sweats, vomiting, chills, or cramps.

Judging the Level of Blood Loss

When a vampire feeds on a human, it will usually drink anywhere from one to three pints of blood. The human body holds an average of twelve pints of blood, so that amount is not necessarily life-threatening. However, a vampire might feed off a victim multiple times, and other vampires might also feed off an abducted victim. A person who has suffered an attack could find that he or she has lost close to half of his or her blood.

Medically speaking, there are four levels of blood loss:

Class 1: Loss of up to 15 percent of total blood volume (less than 2 pints). The victim is conscious, speaking, mostly mobile but perhaps slightly dizzy. This is usually no major threat in a healthy person over ninety pounds. Children, elderly people, and the sick might suffer worse effects.

Class 2: This is a loss of 15 to 30 percent of the body's blood volume (about 2 to 3.5 pints, which looks like a hell of a lot if spilled on the floor). This probably won't require a transfusion, but an IV saline solution is a good idea. The pulse rate will rise and the victim's skin might become cool and pale as the body draws in blood from peripheral regions to keep volume going to major organs. The victim might get lethargic or agitated.

Class 3: Trouble—this is a loss of up to 40 percent of the victim's circulating blood volume. This calls for immediate transfusion and IV saline solution. The victim will experience rising heart rate at the same time that blood pressure drops, and then shock and confusion as the capillaries of peripheral tissues don't refill. Shock is a critical situation.

Class 4: Fatal—the loss of over 40 percent of blood volume, upwards of five or six pints. The body has no compensation for this, and shock, brain swelling, organ failure, and death will ensue if a blood transfusion is not rapidly administered.

Vampire Fact:

Two main forms of German vampires have been identified: the *Nachtzehrer* ("nightwaster"), and, in southern Germany, the *Blutsauger* (literally, "bloodsucker"). *Nachtzehrers* were similar to Slavic vampires, in that those people who suffered traumatic deaths, in accidents or as suicides, were often at greatest risk for vampirism and would return from the grave to feast on the living. *Blutsaugers* were described as pale, somnambulant revenants.

Because the blood that was lost is sloshing around in some vampire and not on the floor, judging blood loss isn't easy, and you'll have to depend on the degree of critical symptoms. Is the victim's heart rate up but blood pressure dropping? Is the person extremely pale or cool to the touch? Are the symptoms of hypovolaemic shock present (hypertension, rapid and weak pulse, shallow respiration, cool skin, altered mental state, or great anxiety)? If these general criteria are met, start a transfusion as quickly as possible. You won't have a chance to test the transfused blood for disease, but that's just how it's going to be in these emergency situations.

Important note: Write your blood type in indelible marker on your body somewhere—your arm, chest, or ankle. This way, a quick transfusion can be had if you're unconscious (assuming there's someone on hand with your blood type who can give you blood).

Vampire Fact:

The first vampire epidemic in Serbia occurred in the late 1720s (the country was under Turkish rule at the time) and began with a farmer named Arnold Paul. Paul, a veteran who claimed to have been attacked by a vampire while fighting in conflicts in what was then called Turkish Serbia, died in 1727 in an accident. Three weeks after his burial, four people claimed to have seen him, and when those four people died a panic began. Town officials opened Paul's grave, and his body appeared fresh, as witnessed by two military surgeons. The investigating party stabbed Paul's body, and the wound bled profusely. The investigators staked the body, beheaded Paul, and then cremated him, doing the same to the four people who had claimed to see him.

Infection with Vampire Blood

The effects of drinking vampire blood will not be seen immediately. Most victims who are given vampire blood have been drained of half or more of their own blood (low blood volume seems to be a necessary precondition of transformation), and while the introduction of vampire blood will sustain them, they will seem to have fallen into a deep unconsciousness or coma. Vampires that usually convert a victim do so after abducting them, and your chances of finding this person before the transformation begins are slim. But there will be those undead that randomly give their blood to victims, in some kind of quest to turn every human into a vampire. To determine if the victim was in fact given vampire blood, look for these signs:

- Coma-like state with extremely faint, erratic pulse and minimum blood pressure that lasts for several days before regaining consciousness.
- Upon regaining consciousness, periods of confusion and agitation followed by sleepiness and lethargy.
- Somnambulism, loss of appetite, cramps, lack of interest, delusion.

Medication Combinations for Fighting Vampirism

Combinations of vasoconstrictive medications with anticonvulsant drugs (such as the migraine medication Topamax) have shown in some tests to slow the rate of infection.

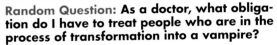

Random Question: As a doctor, what obligation do I have to treat people who are in the process of transformation into a vampire?

Put simply, you have an obligation to stop it, although you cannot be legally held responsible for failing to do so (various laws will be passed to that effect). Perhaps the most important part of the modern Hippocratic oath as it applies to the victim of the vampire is, "I will prevent disease whenever I can." In other words, the doctor must attempt to stop full-blown vampirism. Of course, the real conundrum will be whether you can take time away from human victims in need to try to halt vampiric transformation, given that by the time you actually have a victim before you, he will likely be well past victim state and actively becoming a vampire. There will be a kind of triage you will have to apply.

Vampire Fact:

In his landmark book *The Vampire in Lore and Legend* (1961), Montague Summers related a story from Russian folklore in which a man traveling in the country at night halts a vampire from returning to its grave before sunrise and demands it to tell him how to resurrect the two young boys the vampire had drained. The vampire tells the man to take the left skirt of its burial shroud and put it into a pot with three hot coals, and then leave the two dead children in a room with the smoking pot, closing the door. The man allows the vampire to return to its grave before sunrise, and then goes to the home of the children with the piece of shroud. The children do, indeed, breathe in the smoke of the burning shroud and revive.

Vasoconstrictors slow the circulatory system, and anticonvulsants reduce excitatory nerve impulses while opening stabilizing channels in the nervous system. This slows the delivery of the virus to the cells. Mood-altering medications such as Xanax and Zoloft have little impact compared to anticonvulsants.

Complete Blood Transfusion

This might sound like the first thing you should do, as it seems simple, but completely draining someone of all the blood they contain (human and vampire) and then filling them with new human blood is deathly dangerous and hard to do without medical training. You can't remove too much blood too quickly, or flood the victim with blood from the donor. The process takes upwards of ten hours, as you basically replace all the victim's blood with completely new blood, an overlapping process that draws down the concentration of vampire blood to zero. You can't move a unit of blood into the bloodstream faster than you can take it out. There is a high risk of contamination and disease. You're going to need more than one donor of the correct blood type, because you can't ever take either the victim's or donor's blood level to a dangerous low point. Note that his process does not remove the virus, just the vampiric blood interacting with the virus.

You will have to go in stages: Remove two units, add two units; remove, add. You will be removing an ever-decreasing concentration of vampire blood per unit, and thus will have to remove upwards of thirty to forty units to remove it all from the victim's bloodstream. Most likely, you won't get it all, but you should get enough that treatments with some medications will inhibit any transformation.

Of course, you can't medicate a victim that you're transfusing—you'll just be removing the medications. So transfuse first, completely, and then watch for any signs of transformation, and then treat with drugs.

And while you're performing this field surgery, you'll also be fighting off vampires, tallying your stores, communicating with your contacts, burning dead vampires, and trying to get four or five hours of sleep (to say nothing of the usual family stresses and bad habits).

Having fun yet?

Vampire Fact:
Unlike that of the neighboring Balkans, true Hungarian folklore is pretty light on indigenous vampire tales (often, stories from neighboring regions, or from previous, historic sections of Austria-Hungary, are incorrectly ascribed to the country as it is now). But Hungarian lore does contain a *loogaroo*-like being called a *lidérc*. This demonic spirit existed in any form it hypnotized its victim into seeing—a woman, man, a shining ball of light, or some kind of animal. The *lidérc* consumed its victims sexually, killing them through exhausting intercourse.

Random Question: Can I inject myself with vampire blood and take on vampire-like strength without turning into a vampire, assuming I don't have the virus?

Steroids not working, eh? What you're talking about is an extreme risk. There is not yet a blood test to see if you carry the vampire virus, though development for such a test is underway. But without knowing for sure that you *don't* carry the virus, self-administering vampire blood for any reason is a kind of condemnation.

However, for the sake of discussion, let us assume that you are healthy and don't have the vampire virus. An injection of vampire blood would be similar to a transfusion of the completely wrong blood type, like getting B negative when you're A positive. When this happens, you can suffer a serious immune response that destroys red blood cells and causes a drop in blood pressure and possibly death. If you don't have an allergic reaction, a significant dose of vampire blood will disable you for a day or two; you'll feel sluggish, nauseous, and dizzy, and be *completely useless*.

And after this ludicrous experiment, you also will contain every viral and bacterial element that the vampire had, possibly typhus, smallpox, cholera, encephalitis, and bubonic plague.

Tough list to choose from, eh?

Quarantines

The word *blood* is going to be spoken ad infinitum in the coming days. So much paranoia will spill over that in many places, self-appointed safety directors, sheriffs, and general vigilantes are going to go on unrestrained patrols, day and night, looking for anyone acting weird in the slightest.

Try acting ***not*** weird and see how far you get.

Rounding up and taking into custody people suspected of being infected or suffering early stage transformation will probably take place in many towns and counties, although its legal ramifications most likely will not have been worked out sufficiently before the uprisings begin. Who has the authority to do this? Cops? And where will they put everyone?

Worst-case scenario: We have a Guantanamo-like operation in every other town, fueled by plague paranoia.

But what about the small team of friends or a family, or the individual fighting to stay alive—what should they do when they face a transforming victim/rising vampire and have no means to help? That's a tough call.

Handling Infected Humans

For safety's sake, assume that victims who have been fed upon by a vampire have also imbibed vampire blood. This might be a bit unfair, but in dire situations, it might be the only reasonable reaction.

In a housebound setting with multiple members, simply monitor the person's health. Watch for the signs described here. If you ultimately determine that the person has been bitten but has not ingested vampire blood, then you're somewhat in the clear, although you now have an elevated concern: This person will certainly transform once given the blood of the undead. That does make them a bit of a risk. In a family or true team setup, you must simply provide better cover for this person. He or she is an increased responsibility, and that is that. Would you like to be so at risk? No. So, watch his or her back as best you can.

If a person in your home or apartment does begin to transform and you've no medicines or transfusion capabilities, you're facing the inevitable. There are a few things you can do to forestall full vampirism. But, ultimately, you'll have a vampire on your hands. (It's always the middle child, isn't it?)

Now, let's say you're pretty much on your own—you can't trust anyone around you because you've hooked up with some real wackos and you've little influence over decision making or medical treatments of infected and transforming individuals, or you're simply rambling and hiding, going solo. What's a gun-toting loner to do with all these blood-feast victims?

There's little that can be done with limited means. If you find yourself in bad company, you might be forced to lock up raving humans transforming into vampires—or those just about there—for your own safety. It is a regrettable necessity. As for the infected, help them as best you can; you just might keep vampire numbers down. Being in proximity to an infected person does not present a hugely heightened danger, as a vampire will not be able to tell the victim is infected until it actually bites that person. Infected people are not any more likely to attract a vampire than your average twenty-five-pounds-overweight American.

Legal Ramifications of Quarantines

Finding people who have been infected but untouched by vampire blood and locking them up poses all kinds of questions. Can you say it's for their safety? Or is this unconstitutional? Is it just lock-and-key paranoia or practical decisiveness? Perhaps the biggest questions of all are: Is it okay to simply toss *habeas corpus* out the window? Do life, liberty, and the pursuit of happiness cease to be functional ideals during vampire uprisings?

You might be able to rationalize the locked-room protection of an infected family member, if this decision is arrived at by family consensus, and a sibling, adult, or cousin is put in a secure place for their own safety at night. This can be considered the "better cover" mentioned above.

But when security forces or vigilantes snatch a free citizen after the "Bite Inspection Committee" has made its rounds, you've got a different situation. Taking "at risk" individuals out of the community at large and stashing them in "secure" places can easily be classified as illegal imprisonment, the very thing the writ of *habeas corpus* is supposed to prevent or remedy. With the inevitable suspension of the writ during the most intense periods of nation-wide vampire attack, legal arguments against imprisonment will be tough to mount. Secondarily, such action would create a concentration of infected persons in one small place, and were vampires to find out about their location—a virtual certainty—then you've turned these victims into a group of sitting ducks who will surely see their "protectors" run for cover when a gang of hungry vampires breaks into the minimum security prison.

Vampire Fact:

In Nigerian folklore, vampire-like witches from the Niger River area can—through invisible, nonphysical means—suck the blood of a victim without the victim feeling pain (or perhaps feeling the pain but not discerning a reason for the pain). This is similar to the astral vampires described by Western occultists. Also in Africa, the Ashanti people of Ghana speak of a vampire-like creature called an *asasa-bonsam*. This creature looks like a person but has teeth made of iron. It will wait in the deep jungle with its legs dangling down from a tree limb so it can use its hooked feet to catch someone passing below.

What to Do About Bites If Alone

The lone rambler in the time of vampire uprisings has either got to be desperate, crazy, or *one serious badass mofo*. Sure, maybe you're bionic or you think you've learned a lot reading the Harry Potter books. Hell, maybe you're freakin' Storm from the X-Men. But one thing is for sure: The loner, outdoors, is going to get bitten. Here are a few tips:

Carry a Proper First-Aid Kit

At least have the ability to clean and sterilize a bite mark and other minor wounds when in the field alone.

This, of course, assumes that you survive the process of being captured and bitten. In some cases you might face a vampire that ambushes you and gets in a quick bite, sucks, and leaves. But other times, you will be fed upon viciously and continuously, and assaulted in all the worst ways. (See the first-aid kit detailed in chapter 3.)

If you find that you've been badly bitten and drained of much blood, do your best to find shelter in which to recover. But movement will be severely hindered by significant blood loss. You will become terrifically thirsty. Do not guzzle down your water, or whatever water that you find; rehydrate slowly and steadily, and take a salt tablet (pickle brine, a stand-by of football-team trainers, also works in small doses).

Resist Temptation

Surrounded by vampires that have fed off you, you might come to the realization (if you're still conscious) that the only way to survive at all is to ask for transformation into a vampire. That's an extremely difficult decision, with all sorts of ethical and personal ramifications.

But there's another issue for the solo traveler: Once having seen vampires in the open and witnessed their abilities, how do you prevent yourself from succumbing to the temptation to voluntarily become a vampire? Many lone travelers have given in because of fear, exhaustion, a sense of the inevitable, and a desire for vampiric power.

While all sorts of anti-vampire legislation will be ramrodded through Congress by numerous politicians—making entering the country as a vampire a federal crime, making the drinking of blood a felony, and making the willful transformation into a vampire, either of yourself or another, a capital offense—the process of becoming a vampire can't really be viewed as a crime, nor is the vampiric state wholly unnatural.

But you certainly won't be *you* anymore.

You will entirely abandon your life as you know it, leaving behind those who love you (*ahem*, wherever they are).

This book and its publisher advise adamantly against ever becoming a vampire voluntarily. It is a vicious and horrendous, animal-like existence, and it won't stop for a long, long time. It is a "life" driven entirely by hunger, desire, and fear at nearly unbearable levels.

Vampire Fact:
From the lands that are now the Czech Republic and Slovakia come two remarkable stories of vampires unaffected by staking. In the 1300s, after a number of deaths in Blau, a Bohemian village, residents disinterred and staked the suspected vampire, but he thanked them for giving him a weapon he could use to protect himself and sent them away with his laughter. After sundown, he unstaked himself and continued his lethal rounds; his former neighbors died a week after his nocturnal visit. Cremation finally ended the vampire's terrors, after he killed several more people. Then, in 1345, a dead woman thought to have been a witch assumed an animal form and terrorized the town of Lewin. Uncovered and staked, she arose at night, and, in human form, used the stake to defend herself as she again attacked the villagers. Again, fire was the only effective means of destruction.

Mental Combat with the Rising Vampire

Somewhere between determining that a person has been infected with vampire blood and the visual signs of transformation, you might try a relatively safe 50-percent blood transfusion and then administer some anticoagulant and anticonvulsant medications, and you just might hinder the virus enough that it never fully takes hold in the victim, and the human immune system will be able to carry the rest. If you pull this off, it is indeed Miller Time (or, for you Oregonians, Dead Guy Time).

Or, let's say you fail. You'll need a drink, then, too. If you've got antipsychotics on hand, try them, and begin a very determined form of psychological warfare with the vampiric mentality that is blossoming in your former friend, sibling, spouse, or gunnery sergeant (good God—*vampire marines*?). Even if you don't have the meds, play the mind games for as long as you can—you might at least secure in the vampire's mind a sense of responsibility to or respect for those who populated its human world. *The life you save might be your own.*

The Power of Persuasion

A transforming victim who has regained consciousness is not fully aware of his vampire self inside. While his new mentality will take many cues from his body, you can interfere with those signals a good deal in the early stages, assuming you're sure this person is, in fact, transforming.

You must try to persuade him that the strange feelings he's having derive from his terrible physical state. Don't tell him that his feelings are wrong—he'll simply resist you. But give him several very concrete reasons why he feels the way he does: blood loss, dehydration, and injury. If he asks if he's turning into a vampire, tell him, "No." This is no time to get caught up in a "patient's bill of rights," and you're no doctor—you're trying to slow down the arrival of a being that might kill you.

The more detailed an explanation you can give for what the victim is experiencing, the better the effects of your argument will be, especially if he develops a distinct fear that he is, indeed, transforming. Recount the circumstances of his attack and rescue, and tell him succinctly how you believe he was not fully infected: "There was no vampire blood on you, not in your mouth or on your lips." Resurfacing memories of drinking vampire blood can be explained by saying that the mind tries to control what it fears most through dreams.

Tell him that the attack and grasp of a vampire can fill a victim with so much fear that the person can sometimes become deluded into thinking that he *is* a vampire, but any such feelings must be ignored. Continued physical problems can be associated with blood loss, especially if a transfusion was necessary.

Continue this persuasive discussion for as long as you can. The victim will reach a point when his mind begins to respond fully to the physiological messages he's getting and then he won't have to ask if he might be turning into a vampire—on a conscious level he will know for a fact that he is different. But even then, there are other arguments that can be made.

Assertion of Identity, Association, and Place

The transforming human, on the cusp of becoming a vampire, will begin to wonder about her individual status: "What am I?" she'll ask. During this time, you must constantly remind her of her human identity. Show her photographs (especially those of the victim and other people together), videos, her birth certificate, passport, and driver's license—anything that serves as an original record of her true self. Friends should speak of events and actions in the past that conjure the victim and others, putting them in a specific place and time. Recount major narratives of her past. Dated, handwritten letters by and to the victim help greatly to rekindle memories of past places, people, and times. If you have it, show the victim a copy of her résumé, emphasizing business associations and membership in social organizations. If the victim is an artist or musician, show her copies of her work, play her music, or give her musical instruments and remind her of the numerous other artists she knows and likes. You must counter every instance that the victim asks, "What am I becoming?" or "Could I be turning into a vampire?" with a photograph, a letter, a story—anything that reaffirms her human life and personhood.

Deception

This is a measure of last resort, a kind of operative denial. Refuse the victim's vampiric advances and chide him for acting in such a way. Demand that he resume his role in the family or team; help him and encourage him to take up his former duties. Remind him of the need to help quell and kill marauding vampires.

Yes, you are postponing the inevitable, assuming that medicinal treatments and partial or complete blood transfusion could not be attempted. But what you are also doing is giving yourself time to create a place where your vampire friend or family member can be secured—locked away somehow—to await further attempts at reducing or denaturing his vampire state.

Housing a New Vampire Securely

There's a good chance it will happen: Someone close will become a vampire, and you can't just let this person run out into the night. The right of citizen's arrest doesn't extend to taking prisoners, but in this case, you're going to have to push the extralegal limits of the situation.

Locking Down the Subject

Forget ropes for securing a vampire. You're going to need handcuffs, shackles, chains, and padlocks. Lock the vampire to the floor, if possible, in a small room or closet where most people in the house don't have to go. This will be much more difficult in an apartment or residence hall. Don't lock a vampire to a chair or other furniture that she can move or break. A bed frame that can be bolted to the floor or even

A properly restrained
person going through
transformation

a heavy piece of exercise equipment such as a Universal home gym can work as an anchor point. Cuff the wrists and shackle the ankles.

You'll need to do this before the transformation is complete. A fully transformed vampire won't let you lay a hand on her—you'll get punched, cuffed, or otherwise knocked across the room, and soon tackled and bitten.

Feeding the Subject

The big problem will be feeding the prisoner vampire. You can try animal blood, if you've got any animals you can successfully bleed, like a cow. Otherwise, you're going to have to ration human blood, just enough to keep the vampire alive.

Feeling gross?

Vampire Fact:
In the folklore of numerous European cultures, and some Asian and African traditions, suicide has a strong connection to vampirism. While drunkenness, a violent personality, and association with witchcraft can also make a person vulnerable to the vampire, the suicide victim frequently comes back to haunt friends and family as a member of the undead. This is a prominent feature in the vampire tales of the Balkans, Romania, and Russia.

Random Question: Let's say that a family member who is now a vampire proves to be trustworthy and stays in the home. How do you prevent other vampires from sensing his presence and coming for him?

The trustworthy family vampire is a known phenomenon in the history of vampirism. And you are right: There is a good chance that other, roving vampires that attempt to enter the house might sense him there, through their refined senses of smell or taste. A live vampire gives off a scent recognized by others.

To prevent trouble, as much as possible, confine your family vampire to a central room, away from outer walls. Keep him away from windows. You can mask his scent to a degree with a paste of wood ashes and Vaseline, but there are only so many times you can do that practically, although it's a good idea when numbers of vampires are moving through, as during the height of the uprising in your area.

Aside from that, give him something blunt with which he can defend himself: a crowbar, bat, or pipe. But don't arm him with a blade or gun; that's too risky.

Of course, having a truly loyal vampire on your side in a fight is quite a plus. His strength and senses can significantly elevate the efficacy of your security efforts. But a vampire that is discovered to have tried to kill other vampires, for the sake of protecting humans, is a marked bloodsucker. Eventually, teams or entire covens will seek out and attempt to destroy him.

When the vampire attacks are over, you will have to help sustain a totally new form of "living" for your vampire brother or sister. That's another book entirely.

Is Imprisonment Worth the Effort?

During imprisonment, you can attempt to continue to reason with the vampire and secure his promise that he won't turn violent or murderous. But there's really no way to tell if he'll keep his promise until you unshackle him. Some highly conscientious vampires that arose from very family- or friend-connected situations might be able to keep the promise. Most others, in the grip of their new existence, will be unable to resist taking human blood.

Imprisonment might not be possible under the crazy circumstances of active vampire attack in your neighborhood or town. A transformed friend might simply dash off into the night, or he might set his sights on you. In fact, in most cases, you will simply have to abandon the transforming victim, as there is nothing you can do, unless you are, in fact, tough enough to shoot him.

What to Do If You're in a Relationship with a Vampire

Among the numerous social and personal upheavals that come with a widespread vampire attack, you might find yourself in the awkward and complicated situation of being involved with a member of the undead. Crazier things have happened, like Lance Armstrong dating an Olsen twin (even the vampires can't tell those girls apart). The possibility of a spouse or boyfriend or girlfriend getting turned into a vampire is not so remote that you don't have to consider it. Americans who find themselves in a living/undead relationship will have to ask some tough questions and make some tough decisions. Maybe you've already done a little vampire role-playing—in a game, in the bedroom, or in your shrink's office—but now you're in for the real thing.

Could You Stay Married to or in Love with a Vampire?

The extent of your personal, emotional, and legal connections to the vampire is your first consideration. For the married or single person very much in love with someone unfortunate enough to have been transformed, a lot will hinge on the behavior of the vampire and the level of trust in the human in the relationship.

If the vampire is somehow capable of living a relatively "human" lifestyle—no serial feasting or killing, no extended travel or roaming, no joining covens—he or she might be able to keep up his or her end of the relationship, albeit at night. And if the human spouse or significant other can tolerate a mostly nocturnal relationship, a few odd changes in his or her mate's appearance, and the necessity of containing and presenting the main food supply to the undead partner, well, then the relationship might last. But, yes, you're going to be lightheaded a lot, because your mate's blood-feeding habits will have to be kept hush-hush once the vampire horde has been put down, and there's only so much cow blood you're going to be able to buy or get for free before people start to wonder (slaughterhouse blood sales may even be made illegal, in a reactionary crackdown on lingering vampirism).

But living a so-called human lifestyle is extremely difficult for most vampires, new or old. Their bloodlust is too strong.

Do You Live Together?

Living with a vampire mate might actually be a bit easier on the human partner, as you're there to keep an eye on the beloved bloodsucker and help with vampiric needs. And if the vampire partner stays in, for both safety's sake and the sanity of the human partner, then living together might be easiest, as your daytime-nighttime schedules will overlap quite a bit.

But if you live with a vampire that prefers or needs to go out at night, you'll find that living together is a bit of a strain. You might sense the vampire needs to have time away from you, or you have a hunch she wants to meet other people. Going out with your vampire partner is just about out of the question. If she has vampire associates, they will immediately be suspicious of a human in their midst. And you won't be allowed to go to the locations that "good vampires" go to, in their doubly underground lifestyle.

What Is Your Level of Trust?

How would you react to the following statements from a vampire spouse or significant other?

"I know I was gone from sundown to sunup, but all I drank was monkey blood."

"They're just friends—they're *not* a coven."

"I'm cool just playing Xbox at the blood orgies."

"Transform a sixteen-year-old cheerleader into a vampire? *Me*?"

"Who told you I go to an all-boy Brazilian coven?"

"I am *not* five hundred years old."

Random Question: I shot a few vampire in-laws and this has created a really awkward situation with my husband's family. How can I fix this?

Yes, that is indeed awkward. Can't you just hear the comments at Thanksgiving a few years from now? "Well, dessert was pretty good, but it's nothing like the pumpkin pie Aunt Marjorie would have made, if your wife hadn't *shot her* during the vampire uprising!"

Blood is, indeed, thicker than saving your own ass, isn't it?

The person that you'll mostly have to deal with about this is your husband, and given that his wife is still alive and doing things around the house, much to his benefit, what's he got to complain about? *Nothing.* You might just have to ask him to take sides—you, or the rest of his reindeer-sweater-wearing family.

If you can't socialize alongside your vampire partner, you're simply going to have to take his word for it that what he says he did (or didn't do) is the truth. You'll have a hard time proving anything, as vampire friends don't squeal on vampire friends. Believing in your vampire mate who claims to care about you isn't going to be easy.

What Are You Willing to Endure?

One big, obvious fact is that eventually your vampire partner is going to realize that she is going to outlive you by several hundred years, assuming all goes well. No amount of BOTOX and surgery is going to keep you in shape as you stand beside your unchanging beloved. You're going to be sixty, and your mate is going to be getting text messages from twenty-year-olds.

You're also going to have to consider the reaction of your family and friends. Think of how this extended period of vampirism is going to change the way Americans think of outsiders and one another. So your people are eventually, and quite quickly, going to catch on that your paramour is a bloodsucker. And then what? "I don't want that leech in my house!" "How will we explain it to Nana?" "You're doing this just to spite us." And so on.

Some families will certainly be a bit more accepting, especially those that already have a vampire member. But those who lost loved ones to vampire attack will most assuredly hold a grudge.

Then there are all the personal things: No sunlit picnics. Cooking for one. The immense job of obtaining and maintaining a legal blood supply. A sex life that sometimes seems like something out of a bad Cinemax movie. The nocturnal comings and goings. The great difficulty of explaining why Mommy or Daddy isn't around when the kid gets up for school.

It's an immensely stressful arrangement and one few humans and vampires can endure.

Moving on from the Vampire Affair

The subtitle of this book is *How to Fight, and Win, Against the Undead*, and for the most part, that idea, and this book, is about (violent) self-defense against attacking vampires. But there is also the inner self-defense one needs against the loss of a partner to the vampire world.

This is no ordinary breakup. It's somewhere between divorce and death. You will in all probability never see this person again. And you know that she is being absorbed into a terrifically dangerous and difficult existence. Most new vampires do not survive their first year among the undead. It is extremely difficult to let go of someone under these circumstances. There is a terrific amount of grief that must be dealt with.

The relationship will also mark you for life, no pun intended (OK, pun intended). Many who knew of your vampire spouse or lover will hold that against you (think of the French men and women who, after the Allied liberation, were ostracized for previously associating with Nazis). You will also have some difficulty explaining your affair to a future partner. The post-vampire relationship will be fraught with insecurities and misunderstandings if the new partner finds out about your former fling with a member of the undead.

Vampire Fact:
Among the pre-Buddhist beliefs of the Thai people was the presence of *phi*, which were the ghosts of people who had died suddenly, were killed by animals, did not have a proper burial, or had died in childbirth. The *phi* roamed the countryside and sometimes carried out vampire-like attacks. Young men were the targets of *Phi Song Nang*, which assumed the form of beautiful women who attacked the men and sucked their blood.

Chapter 3

Your New Job: Killing Vampires

Depending upon where you live, you might see a few vampires only during periods of increased vampire activity. In other places you will witness a significant onslaught, based on numerous variables: the quantity of healthy, worthy victims in a given place; easily hunted, isolated populations of humans; numerous structures or places where vampires can hide during the day; and the presence or absence of military forces or police.

But given the overall increase of vampire predation on humans, you face a significant chance of having to resist and destroy a number of vampires. There could be two- or three-week periods in which you must defend your home, family, and friends through the night and take measures to fortify your home during the day. Knowing that a multi-vampire attack could be around the corner, you need to have the stuff to last.

Scared, or Prepared?

At some point in this period of vampire attacks, so many uprisings will occur across the country that the usual American business week is going to be significantly disrupted; there might be weeklong periods of reduced productivity and slowed movement of goods in certain areas or sections of the country. The president will most likely declare a national state of emergency (a significant legal development, post 9/11). In many ways, this vampire epidemic will be like the aftermath of a hurricane, just without the massive property damage, but with the temporary confusion, chaos, and disruption.

However, the crisis will actually provide a boost to the retail market in the beginning, because you're going to need a bunch of stuff; only later will the economy suffer the costs of humans putting in so much time resisting vampire attack. Don't waste your money on the folksy and religious tchotchkes. Of course, there will be a run on fresh garlic—it'll probably go up to fifteen dollars a clove—no matter that it doesn't work. You want some real, effective hardware, and the basic necessities in significant quantities.

Water

Bottled water, tap water, well water—whatever. Store at least sixty gallons of it in the beginning of the combat, but one hundred gallons is better. You can go twenty days without food before your anti-vampire performance will really start to suck (ha!). Four days without water and you will be on the floor, dying a very crampy death. Personal hygiene will be important, and you'll need water for this, mainly for brushing your teeth, washing your hands, sterilizing wounds, and cleaning off blood and gore. The rest of you can stink for a while. Ration your stored water in times of continual attack—you don't know how much more you'll be able to obtain if localized vampire combat carries on for some time and municipal water systems suffer breakdowns, largely due to lack of personnel. Those of you with wells can probably get away with more liberal usage. But when water sources are in question and bloodsuckers abound, you can have two pints of water a day for drinking, and a cup for brushing your teeth and washing your hands.

Nonperishables

Anything in cans or wrapped in foil wrappers that doesn't need refrigeration, as well as freeze-dried food, MREs, and anything pickled, will last for a while. Purchase high-protein, high-energy foods—read the labels and get foods that hit the 8 percent daily value mark for protein and 24 percent for carbs. Black beans, kidney beans, chickpeas, and black-eyed peas are prime choices.

Forget the "empty calories" of potato chips, Doritos, Little Debbie cakes, and the like. Everything you eat in this emergency period has got to do something for you: give you energy, give you the stuff you need to keep your tissues repaired and healthy, and give your brain enough sugar to think clearly (your brain pretty much runs on blood sugar, and natural sugars occur in all good foods). The only indulgence that's legit, as we all know, is chocolate, the darker the better, because that actually provides some nutrition.

Give yourself two meals a day: when you awaken (you're going to have to sleep sometime), and at the midpoint of your shift. You don't need any food as you approach your downtime.

Hungry? Think about drinking blood.

First-Aid Kit

Most injuries and wounds are going to be bad cuts, bone fractures, burns of varying degrees, and, of course, puncture wounds. So a good first-aid kit should contain:

- Forceps, scissors, tweezers, a small, sharp knife or scalpel, suture kit, latex gloves.
- Acetaminophen (10 tablets), ibuprofen (10 tablets), aspirin (20 tablets), bismuth (antidiarrheal;12 tablets), basic antibiotics (20 tablets), salt supplements (30 tablets).
- Iodine (one 8-ounce bottle), hydrocortisone cream,

Neosporin or other antibiotic ointment, surgical soap (1 bar), nasal spray (1 bottle), sterile eyewash, 30+ SPF sunscreen, bug spray (at least 12 percent DEET).

- Superglue (for closing wounds; one tube), medicated membrane dressings (in various sizes), sterile bandages (multiple types in various sizes), sterile adhesive bandages, small adhesive bandages (for small cuts or fingers), gauze rolls (at least 6), surgical tape (3 rolls), duct tape (1 roll), sterile towels or paper towels.

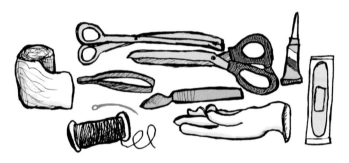

But don't waste any of this stuff. Minor cuts, including those that bleed a good bit but don't need stitches, simply need to be cleaned with soap and water and then covered until the bleeding stops. After that, uncover small wounds to the air to let the a scab form.

You can sew? Then you can put in stitches. Know how to use superglue? Then you can close bad cuts if you don't know how to sew. And only the most culturally sheltered people (and Smith graduates) don't know how to use duct tape, so you can use that to make splints. About the only skill that you seriously might need that isn't too common is the ability to perform a direct blood transfusion for those who have been fed upon heavily by vampires.

One note about blood: Human and vampire blood is toxic. It carries everything from HIV/AIDS to Chagas' disease to the flu. In dire situations, when someone is bleeding profusely or has been bled by a vampire, getting type-correct blood into that person is the absolute priority. You also won't have the means to test for diseases in donor blood. You're going to have to go on faith that the donor (and that

Vampire Fact:
A second vampire epidemic in Serbia in the late 1720s into the early 1730s extended from the Arnold Paul case. Four years after Paul was staked, beheaded, and cremated along with four of his victims, seventeen people seemingly died of vampirism over three months in the same area Paul had roved as a vampire. An Austrian military surgeon, Johannes Fluckinger, led an investigation that focused on a recently deceased man named Milo, who reportedly had attacked a young girl at night. Milo's body was disinterred and found to be in an undecomposed state. Fluckinger decided on a thorough course of action: Stake and burn Milo, then disinter everyone in the town who had died recently and examine them. Of forty people who were exhumed, seventeen were found in undecomposed states, and these were also staked and burned. Fluckinger determined, strangely, that four years earlier Arnold Paul had fed on and somehow vampirized a number of cows, and recently deceased people had somehow risen and fed off these cows. In 1732 Fluckinger presented a report to the Austrian emperor, and its published edition was widely circulated.

might be you) is disease-free.

Tool Kit

If you're a carpenter, mechanic, plumber, or contractor, you've probably got more tools than you can name. You're all set.

Those of you who can identify a hammer and think you know which end to hold should have a kit with the following: vise grips, wire stripper, wire cutter, crescent wrench, socket wrench, Phillips and flat-blade screwdrivers (multiple sizes), standard pliers, needle-nosed pliers, claw hammer, electric drill with kit of bits, files, a good multitool as backup, and a tape measure.

Mostly, you're going to be using a hammer or power drill to sink nails and screws, respectively, into window frames and doors. Sure, if you've got a DeWalt nail gun, use it, but don't think you'll kill any bloodsuckers with it—not unless you rig it so it shoots a quarter-inch rivet at 1,200 feet per second.

Don't use a power saw of any kind to decapitate dead vampires. You'll simply spray a lot of vampire blood and tissue all over the place, and you'll stand a chance of losing fingers. This is where you need a proper machete, kukri, or ax. "Swing, don't saw," as they said in the vampire epidemic of Serbia in 1730.

Essential Gear

Between military needs and hard-core outdoor enthusiasts, we've got ourselves some damn fine consumer equipment in this country these days. *How did we beat the British Army without this stuff?*

- Hard-wired and battery-powered motion sensors and motion-triggered spotlights: Get a bunch and set them up at all the entry points and corners of your home. Look for 300-watt bulbs and get motion-sensor beams with at least a twenty-five-foot range.
- Hand-operated spotlights: Get yourself several three-million-candlepower spotlights and keep them by doors and windows. You can, in fact, momentarily blind most vampires with that level of candlepower. Don't ever shine this thing on yourself—you won't see clearly for about ten minutes.
- Heavy-duty flashlights and headlamps: Pick a good brand and have a bunch of each kind. Lithium-battery halogen-bulb models are the way to go, though this is pricey stuff. As soon as it gets dark, put your headlamp on your head and leave it there. Many flashlights and headlamps made for hunters now come with green-, blue-, or red-tinted settings. Vampires are very adept at noticing light of any shade, so the color doesn't matter all that much, although the green- and red-tinted light is easier on human eyes

in the dark.

- Night-vision monoculars or goggles: These items are essential, and every store and Web site that offers them is going to sell out, so *buy now*. The Navy SEALs, Green Berets, Delta Force, Rangers, and CIA military ops all have the good stuff (for both the foreign wars and the vampire uprisings at home), but there are some decent models out there for the civilian market. If you have such optics, you'll most likely see your first vampire through a night-vision lens. But there is one drawback: These optics often cut off your peripheral vision. You're looking directly ahead, in a pretty tight field of vision. The tactic here is to have a night-vision spotter who calls out and jacklights the target and a second person to whack the leech.

- GPS: About 60 percent of everyone who bought a GPS unit has yet to figure out how to use it. Buddy, it's time to sit down with the instruction booklet and learn yourself something. Because what you're going to do is put a global tracking chip on every important person in your life and program that into your unit. You're going to have to keep track of your family, friends, and your main people. Don't put it past a freaky longhaired no-good high-school dropout vampire to try to carry off your fifteen-year-old daughter whose friends tell her she looks just like a blond Natalie Portman. Unless a vampire drains its victim completely (which is possible) or injects its own blood into its victim to convert the person, someone who has been bitten and abducted can be located, given a transfusion, and revived. So lock a Teflon GPS bracelet around your teenage daughter's ankle and give her a good talking-to about boys.

* Tactical vest: You want this for the pockets. Organize it with six items, no more, because you won't easily remember more than six. Memorize where you put each item and don't change the pocket you put it in. Have your vest ready at all times in case you have to grab it quickly.

* Crash bag: A small backpack containing a few essentials—extra handgun, ammo, water, small first-aid kit, flashlight, cell phone—that you grab on your way out to your escape route if you have to abandon the house.

* Body armor: Easily reached places on your body that produce a serious blood flow when punctured are your carotid artery in your neck, your brachial artery in your upper arm, and your femoral artery in your thigh. But don't expect to encounter stylish vampires who like to make neat holes and insert jeweled metal spouts and drink with class. *Rougher, hungrier vampires will think nothing of decapitating or dismembering a victim, chopping a hole in your head, or cutting straight into the pulmonary artery to cause maximum blood flow.* So armor

that protects your head, neck, upper body, arms, and your pelvic area and hips ain't a bad thing to have. A lot of SWAT and military armor does a good job for the upper body. A couple places to look for armor are www.galls.com, www.bodyarmorcompany.com, and www.chiefsupply.com (take note, guys, of the Hatch Centurion Thigh/Groin Protection System). You can also check out a lot of paintball-competition sites for some decent armor; this stuff won't stop bullets, but bullets aren't your big concern. If you would rather just wear that nice studded neck choker that the drummer in a German death-metal band gave you in 1994, go ahead.

Weaponry and How to Use It

The one truly effective defense against vampires is to cause massive bodily damage: creating big holes in their chests, immolation, and decapitation. These are the only measures that kill completely.

But immolation and decapitation are a bit difficult. Handling fire as a weapon is dicey, and when's the last time you saw a flamethrower for sale at your local Army-Navy store? Decapitation is a good thing to do to a vampire corpse, but you'll never survive getting close enough to an active vampire to make use of your favorite machete or heirloom Marine Corps combat knife.

Bows, arrows, and crossbows are also worthless. A hunting arrowhead passing through a vampire will not do much lasting damage, unless it completely severs the aorta or brain stem. You didn't make the Olympic archery team, did you? Stringing up another arrow on a recurve, compound, or crossbow takes a bit of time, and rapid reloading of a weapon that holds multiple rounds will be key.

There is really only one weapon that most Americans both possess in numbers and can handle easily that will do the job: the 12-gauge shotgun.

Shotguns

A shotgun functions best in the range at which you will usually encounter a vampire (five feet to fifty yards), and will cycle quickly enough to kill thoroughly within this range. You want a "tactical" shotgun—one built with a shorter barrel for tight spaces—and nothing less than 12-gauge. Put away the pretty little 28; that's for quail.

A "pump-action" shotgun is one that is reloaded manually, by quickly sliding the pump handle, which is fit around the tubular magazine, toward you and then pushing it back. "Semiautomatic" means you get one bang per pull of the trigger and then the gun cycles itself, ejecting the spent shell and reloading. You don't have to pump this gun, just hang on, because the gun uses the force of the fired round to cycle itself, so you're going to get an extra bit of recoil than with a pump. Do not fret about this. *Hug your gun.*

Some exemplary shotgun models: the Remington 870 Express and 870 Marine Magnum (pumps), the Benelli M1 (a semiauto), the Winchester 1300 Defender, the Mossberg 500

Random Question: What's the deal on silver bullets—should I hand-load a few?

The silver-bullet myth has more to do with werewolves than vampires, although if you look way back, there is a strong connection between the two creatures. In some cultures, vampires can supposedly turn into werewolves. And in Eastern European cultures, vampires could be dispatched with a bullet shot into the chest after the leech was exhumed and the coffin opened. But the magical ability of silver bullets seems to be a folkloric concoction for dealing with werewolves, dating back to the French legend of the Beast of Gévaudan.

If you're loading your own ammo, select hollow-points for handguns or carbines that fire handgun ammo. You might make your cartridges a little "hot"—put a little more powder in them than usual. Load shotgun shells with as much buckshot as can be fired sensibly. If your shotgun can cycle three-inch-long shells, use them.

Persuader (both pumps), and the Remington 1100 Tactical (semiauto). Load one of these with 00 or 000 buckshot; if you think your first shot might have to cover some distance, make the last shell that you load a slug round (which holds a big, bulletlike projectile). Shotguns don't take scopes, but your shooting will benefit from something called a "red-dot" sight—a rear sight shaped like a ring with an illuminated red aiming point.

Rifles and Carbines

In nearly every case, you'll be shooting vampires at night at relatively close range. They won't be out in the daytime, and trying to pick them off at night at a distance of, say, one hundred yards won't happen because you most likely won't have an infrared scope, and long-range shots at night are difficult. The only way to pull off a rifle or carbine shot in the dark is when you have a partner put a bright spotlight on a vampire (such as when you're watching over an outdoor trap—see chapter 4). In these cases, you can fire a slug from a shotgun, which should fly accurately up to one hundred yards.

But if you really want something that shoots a bullet try an ArmaLite or Bushmaster carbine, such as a Bushmaster C15 Model 4, or a Springfield M1A SOCOM II. For shorter distances, a very easy-to-use carbine is the Beretta CX4 Storm. This gun shoots 9 mm pistol ammo, which isn't as slammin' as rifle rounds, but the magazines and ammo are easy to find. Just shoot two or three times with hollow-point bullets.

Handguns

The handgun is a weapon of last resort, when the blood-suckers are nearly upon you and the shotgun is empty. Try these:

- Taurus 4510 TKR with the three-inch barrel: Loaded with either five .45 cartridges or .410 shotgun shells, or a mix, this revolver is a workable survival hand-gun. Aim for the leech's throat or chest.

- Smith & Wesson Model 629 revolver in .44 Mag: Load this with hollow points, aim for the head or heart, and hang on when you pull the trigger or you'll throw the gun into the air, it'll land on your head, and the vampires will laugh as they begin to feed off you while you're still out cold.

If you insist on having a semiauto, any .45-caliber pistol from Springfield, Kimber, or Wilson Combat will be fine, but these are very expensive guns when purchased new. Buy used, if you can find them. If you love your Glock, keep on loving it.

When you start to get into the .454- and .500-caliber range with revolvers, you've got a handgun that can be hard to handle, especially if you've got small hands. Bullet choice might matter more. Hollow-point bullets are a must, at a minimum of .38-caliber. Magnum loads are fine if you can still control the gun for follow-up shots.

A note about suppressors: Shooting guns indoors is hell on the ears, and anything you can do to reduce the aural impact of muzzle blast is good. A number of ear-canal inserts, similar to hearing aids, block loud noise but let you hear conversation. But where legal, using suppressors (often called "silencers," which is inaccurate) can be a big help. A shogun blast can be effectively suppressed, as can that of a rifle or pistol. You *can't* silence a revolver—there is no contained firing chamber on a revolver, and much of the noise comes out the sides of the gun as well as the barrel. Suppressors are commercially available in many places, and you can also fashion your own if you've got the know-how. Typing "homemade suppressor firearm" into Google should find workable instructions, and there will probably be a boom in such DIY gun modification during the vampire uprising. Just check the laws in your state. Suppressors are good for only a certain number of shots before they begin to loose effectiveness, and bullet speed also affects them.

Vampire Fact:
A traditional Slavic method of destroying a vampire (one found in its coffin during the day) was to drive a stake of hawthorn, aspen, or oak through its heart, and sometimes also through its head and stomach. Decapitation might also be performed, the head sometimes placed between the feet of the headless corpse before reburial. If a priest was present, he sprinkled holy water around the body and repeated the funeral service.

Cutting Blades

About the only blades that make sense to have at your side in this uprising period are a kukri and a decent ax. Again, you most likely won't ever get close enough to an active vampire to use these as actual weapons, but they are good for the final dispatch of an incapacitated bloodsucker. Plus, they help conserve ammo.

Legalities

In many states, you need a permit to purchase and posses a handgun, and some states also require a long-arms permit. Given that there will be a run on the firearms supply once everyone realizes how widespread and determined the bloodsuckers are, get going on the paperwork now, because the background checks are going to take awhile.

Of course, during the period of full-on vampire attacks, unofficial weapons sales will flourish. No one at the FBI will have time for background checks when they're trying to figure out who has become a vampire.

But the best thing to do is be completely legal. Laws are laws, vampires or no vampires.

Vampire Fact:

A crucifix as a sacred weapon against vampires does not play any formal role in European or international vampire history before the novel *Dracula* was published in 1897. Certainly, priests were involved in vampire interdiction in Europe, but the specific idea of warding off a vampire with a cross or crucifix does not enter into the Western mind until Bram Stoker's tale became a bestseller. Stoker, following medieval beliefs about the origins of vampirism, imagined that Dracula became a vampire through a bond with Satan himself, and mixed into this idea some Roman Catholic notions of the magical applications of religious objects (crosses, crucifixes, relics) imbued with the sacred.

The Survival Lifestyle: Getting Your Groove On

Many people have compared the far-reaching personal changes that will be required of Americans during the vampire uprising as akin to entering a video game or role-playing game. There is, one senses, some excitement among a few Americans about the encroaching undead: The bloodsuckers represent both a challenge and an actual change

Random Question: How hyper can I be about fighting vampires before it becomes detrimental?

If you reach a point where you're obsessed with getting and being amped up, you're missing the larger picture. If you start to use intoxicating means to psyche yourself up, you're already starting to lose your grip. When your aggression starts to extend past the vampires and is meted out on simple stuff, you need to pull back.

The best way to deal with this is through ritual. High-performance athletes will understand this. Pick a specific moment and a specific way in which you summon the fierceness, focus, and fortitude that you know you will need. Meditate on these things; find them in you and bring them to the surface. Once you have and control these traits, let them flow naturally. How far can you let them go before they become disadvantageous? When you start violating house rules, or when you put team or family members at risk heedlessly, or when you refuse to listen to reasoned arguments for doing something differently, then your intensity is detrimental.

In the same way that you turn them on, pick a moment and a method for turning off these combat traits, at least in enough measure that you can bring your intensity down several levels and deal with nonviolent issues reasonably.

from the horrendously taxing yet mundane workaday life our diabolically sophisticated economy now requires of the average employed American.

You might have that attitude. But those with any experience fighting vampire epidemics will tell you that, like war, it will sometimes make you feel like an animal and act like one, too. You don't want to let yourself slip. You must prep yourself mentally as the attacks begin and check in periodically to see what condition your psyche is in as attacks continue.

Staying Alert, Staying Confident

The first key to staying alert is getting enough sleep and food. Long stretches of sleep will be tough to obtain during the most active period of the uprising. And as vampires come closer and attempt to get in your home or apartment,

Vampire Fact:
In earlier times, Bosnians and Serbians ascribed to a Gypsy belief that male vampires that rose from the grave often sought out their former spouses for sexual intercourse, and could thus produce male offspring called *dhampirs*, natural-born vampire hunters that were able to perceive and kill vampires (as does the title character of the anime series *Vampire Hunter D*). Bulgarians called vampire hunters *vampirdzhija*. Such experts used the magical qualities of holy icons to help them perceive and locate resting vampires in their grave sites.

or attack you outright, your confidence will fray. But you can keep both of these personal elements—alertness and confidence—at high levels with some exercises. Keep yourself alert by:

- **Playing chess, poker (not online), or (nonvideo) role-playing games:** Regularly engage in some kind of gaming that keeps your mind sharp and forces you to think quickly. What you don't want to play is something that distracts you completely, like a video game. You want something that keeps you talking to other people, thinking, and moving your hands and eyes, but that lets you also keep an eye on other things.
- **Reading aloud:** Reading can keep you alert, but it can also be absorbing and make you drowsy when you're tired. But reading aloud (not too loud) keeps the electricity flowing in the brain.
- **Doing calisthenics, tai chi, and yoga:** Your workout schedule (you've got one?) is going to take a hit when the undead prowl. But when you feel yourself fading on night watch, try a little stretching or push-ups or tai chi.

To build and maintain confidence:

- **Make regular calls:** Use your phone and CB to check in regularly with your network of neighbors, friends, and professional contacts—first those in your neighborhood, and then those anywhere. Seek out news about the national situation and insights into anti-vampire defenses.

- **Plan for the post-uprising life:** You need to believe in a time when the attacks are over, large numbers of bloodsuckers destroyed, and scared-thin America gains and holds the upper hand. Figure out something you want to do when the trouble is over: take a vacation, host a big cookout, or go back to school. Then let this thing come to mind when boredom or anxiety begin to take over, focus on it, think it through, and use it as a symbol of life returning to normal.

- **Daytime target practice:** Get used to your shotgun and keep the gun limbered up (new firearms tend to be stiff). Learn to trust your abilities with the gun.

- **Group discussions with your family/team:** Keep a regular meeting time for people in the house to vent frustrations or fears in a supportive environment. Assess everyone's mindset and come to the aid of those who are having weak moments. Knowing that your compadres and family members benefit from your support helps you and lets you know who can be depended upon. There will, however, be those who break down under the stress and cease to be functional. Take this in stride and help them as you can. Truckers, nurses, factory workers, and college students—anyone used to weird hours and extensive late-shift work—will adapt quickly to the timely necessities of the epidemic. Nine-to-fivers, anal-retentives, and indignant AARPers will have a hard time with the new schedule.

Using Positive Visualization

Lots of sports psychologists use this, and perhaps you have benefited from it in some other circumstance. Put simply, positive visualization is a way of imagining yourself meeting and overcoming obstacles, one by one, in slow motion, so that you can consider each problem, brainstorm a solution, apply it, assess the outcome, and, based upon that outcome, move on to the next task. Then, eventually, you can string the entire sequence together and play it in your head at full speed. You'll create a series of variations, with each one achieving your final goal. This is not only a confidence booster but also a way of gaining a mental-tactical edge.

Develop positive visualization routines for:

- Killing vampires as they enter singly or in small groups from various windows or doors, doing so alone and with your shooter team.
- Seeing your red-dot sight on a vampire's forehead or chest and pulling the trigger without having to think about it.
- Standing over dead, blasted vampires, as well as vampires stacked in a pyre; picture maximum success and maximum damage inflicted upon the bloodsuckers.
- Designing and setting traps for vampires, and then eliminating the undead caught in them (see chapter 4).
- Making successful escapes from besieged homes using preplanned routes.

- Executing successful daylight returns to abandoned locations and making repairs necessary for inhabiting the space again.

Your Combat Street Name

Most people will end up defending themselves in a place where they are known by friends and neighbors. But if you find yourself having to survive in an unfamiliar location, especially outdoors, you might want to adopt a street name. While you don't want to succumb to illegal or highly unethical behavior, there is a little ol' shooting war going on against vampires and that might necessitate a bit of what might be referred to as "extralegal" behavior: stealing a car, roughing up a drug dealer, selling blood, or waterboarding some information out of someone (the attorney general's OK with it, you know). So you might want to have a simple name that cannot be legally or historically attached to you, like Mike D., Blondie, or Turd Blossom.

Die, Vampire Die . . . Why Won't You Die?

With the bloodsuckers, you want a method of dispatch that is both easy to use and creates maximum results. Modern firearms get you that. The old, folkloric ways of killing vampires might be tempting, as they don't involve as much hardware, but they aren't the way to go. Here's why.

Stake Through the Heart

Originally, staking a vampire was intended to secure the undead to the ground in which it was buried, if interred in a simple grave in a shroud, or to the back of a coffin, so it would be unable to rise to seek blood and would eventually starve. Numerous film variations of *Dracula* suggest that a stake in the heart also kills a vampire. This might be true if the stake damages the vampire's heart so much that it results in near removal of the organ, or the leech bleeds to death. Otherwise, staking isn't a sure thing. You must be certain of the *deadness* in your undead. If you find a resting vampire, shoot it, then decapitate it.

Random Question: Can you trick a vampire into killing himself?

A few vampire characters in literature have been horrified enough by the necessities of vampire existence that they thought of killing themselves, but in reality, vampires have an intense drive to "live" to feed. And a vampire who has had a near-death experience, either as a human before transformation or as a vampire, will do anything to stay out of the clutches of true, clinical death. You're not going to coerce or brainwash a bloodsucker into suicide like you can with your "friends" on Facebook. Even if you find a vampire so depressed at its lot in life that it is verging on great self-hatred, it will never give a human the satisfaction of having manipulated it. The vampire will catch on immediately, and will soon be cheering herself up by playing Hacky Sack with your brainstem. (That's an exaggeration—vampires think Hacky Sack is silly.)

Dousing with Holy Water

This is another distraction of the *Dracula* films. Unless you have a priest bless a jug of kerosene, most liquid has no effect on vampires (but see Drowning, and Acid and Other Chemicals below). If you're a lapsed Catholic and it makes you feel better, sprinkle some holy water around the house, apartment, or camp, while doing your best Father Guido Sarducci imitation.

Exposure to Sunlight

This, indeed, will kill a vampire, due to their extreme solar sensitivity. But it takes a while. A vampire can run a short distance through direct sunlight, or move in direct sunlight under special shrouds. But after about a minute of exposure, a vampire will begin to suffer a rapid sunburn that can become fatal after several hours: The skin will burn off and then the sun will penetrate to vital organs and roast them. You can trap a vampire in the sun, or expose a captured vampire to the sun, and it will slowly die in front of your eyes, you sadistic prig.

Drowning

Like all air-breathing creatures, alive or undead, vampires need gaseous oxygen, as Christopher Lee's Dracula demonstrates at the conclusion of *Dracula, Prince of Darkness* when he falls through some ice and drowns (it

The horrors of direct sunlight exposure

looks kinda like a bad ice-skating accident). A vampire can be drowned, but not immediately or easily. In combat, if you can hold a small or child vampire underwater long enough, it will drown. Or you can secure a vampire underwater execution style, though how you get cement shoes on a bloodsucker is quite a trick. A vampire will last about five times longer underwater than a human will. Keep in mind that a drowned vampire is an intact vampire, and as such can be reanimated later, if found, with mass transfusions of vampire blood. A dead vampire, as far as you should be concerned, is not an *intact* vampire. So forget drowning—it's too problematic and insufficient.

Acid and Other Chemicals

Acid will kill a vampire, theoretically speaking. But you've got to get a lot of acid on the damn thing, and exactly how are you going to get that much acid, and how are you going to find a superblaster water gun made of glass (which hydrochloric acid won't eat)? Chances are, you'll get some acid on yourself as well and die an inglorious death just when you'd had that big breakthrough with your therapist and could see yourself as finally being happy.

The same pretty much goes for other dangerous, flesh-eating chemicals: How are you going to get enough of them and what is an effective, combat-ready method for deploying them on the undead? Plus, have you seen what a really strong alkaloid will do to a parquet floor?

Forget chemical warfare. It's simply too tricky. Sure, if you're running from vampires in the Big Bad Acid and Alkali Chemical Company warehouse, and you see a way to dump a vat of something on the bloodsuckers, give it a whirl. Just be aware that acids eating through anything give off toxic fumes, so, again: possible ignoble death.

Vampire Fact:
In the summer of 1997, Iranian officials caught the man who had been dubbed the "Tehran Vampire." Although twenty-eight-year-old Ali Reza Khoshruy Kuran Kordiyeh did not drink the blood of his nine victims (eight women and one girl), this taxi-driving serial killer *staked* them, after raping and killing them. In front of a crowd of ten thousand Iranians, relatives of the victims meted out some of the 214 lashes to which Kordiyeh had been sentenced, and then he was hanged.

Destroying Covens

Eliminating actual covens, if the hideouts or vampire ranks can all be located, will fall to the military or other security forces. In fact, most emergency planners and military commanders don't want civilians involved in this. But, as they say, this land is your land, and after surviving a major multi-vampire attack on your home, you might be overcome by a few irresistible urges to find the nest of bloodsuckers in your township and do them in. Buford Pusser would be right behind you.

Finding Covens in Daylight

First, you'll have to identify the coven's house or structure. Look for:

- Homes or buildings that were abandoned or empty before the uprising that now appear to have changes made to the exterior, visible signs of bipedal activity around the site, and vampire graffiti or even coven symbols drawn on or carved into the outer walls. Such symbols will be small and in specific places, such as high on an outer wall, near the roof eaves, or over door frames, and will often appear as a mixture of hieroglyphs, Arabic, and Cyrillic lettering.
- Homes or buildings that have new, small structures set out of the way on the property that look like small minarets, guard booths, or wooden bee hives. These are observation posts, each manned by one "daylight vampire" dressed in shrouds. Some of these extend underground. The vampire watches out a small, screened slit, and has the means to warn the vampires inside. (This is an old vampire method used only on new hideouts and is quickly replaced by electronic surveillance.) There will also be watchers within the building. You will not approach unobserved.

Random Question: Might there be a way to get vampires to fight other vampires, or covens to attack other covens?

Vampires fight plenty among themselves, that's for sure. They fight for territory and they fight for dominance within vampire hierarchies. Great, unseen battles will take place while you are hunkered down in your home. We regular folks, however, have virtually no chance at setting vampire against vampire. You're not going to run up to the side of a coven's lair and tag it—"The Sisters of Mercy Coven rules! The Bauhaus Coven sucks!"—and get Sisters of Mercy and Bauhaus to rumble until they're all dead. The only way that human intervention can set vampire against vampire is for cooperating vampire moles to penetrate far enough into a local vampire population to plant false information that might get back to vampire chieftains and cause fights. The CIA and FBI will be attempting this with cooperative or coerced vampires, and they will have some limited success. The more important role of CIA and FBI moles is to try to find out information that can help anti-vampire combat operations.

Destroying a Coven

Do you *have* to do this? Do you really *want* to do this? How much ammunition have you got? How crazy are your friends? You might also put in a call to your shrink and your lawyer, too, just so the former can make sure you're not mistaking this for something that went wrong during potty-training, and the latter can make last-minute changes to your will (the "of soundness of mind" part might be contested).

After that, in the brightest daylight you can wish for, take with you as many heavily armed compadres as you can find, and follow this general outline to starting total bloodsucking chaos (à la the final scene of *The Wild Bunch*):

Wooden structures: Set up three shooting positions with team members armed with carbines, rifles, and anything capable of fast cycling. Put these along the edge of the property. Make sure each team has a clear field of fire toward the building, but also something solid behind which to hide, as the daylight vampire lookouts will begin sniping at you. If you can get vehicles this close to the building, use them as both transport and cover. Start shooting burning arrows into the wooden structure. (Make burning arrows by wrapping the shaft behind the tip with thick strips of cloth that have been soaked in gasoline and partly dried.) Get the building burning and wait for any vampire activity. Feel free to loose as much ammo as you can spare into the building as the fire catches. Don't be surprised if the leeches actually shoot back.

As stated, vampires usually have no interest in guns, as they prefer the enjoyments of their own inherent skills, but under siege they'll use anything in self-defense.

Metal structures (warehouses): Set up your shooting positions, then have two team members in the biggest vehicle they can find—semi, oil truck, or Brinks truck—ram a significant opening in the building. You might want to armor the windshield and windows on this truck, as vampires are bound to start shooting at it. Then get the vehicle out of there (pick someone who really knows how to drive) and open up with your guns.

Brick structures: Same deal with the vehicle, but you're going to need a hell of big, solid one, and the impact is going to seriously stun your driver, so have her and the other team member fitted out in helmets and protective gear—they might have to make a second or third run at it. Of course, if you have access to some decent explosive material, dynamite, or C-4, and know how to use it, send in a nice fat charge on a remote control or robotic car and blast a hole in the wall that way. Then start shooting.

What will happen?

Nothing: This is the most likely result. The vampires will most certainly have built a bunker beneath the main structure and will retreat to it once the fire and shooting start. They will be able to seal this and remain there until dark. Unless you've got some real ordnance, like a rocket launcher or dynamite, you're not busting that open. Your main achievement will have been damaging or destroying the coven's structure, though not the vampires themselves. However, you'll probably enjoy some serious vampire activity over the next several nights as a swarm of seriously pissed-off bloodsuckers tries to get back at the humans in that area. The locals will love you.

Return fire: Many vampires will have had military training or combat experience at some point in their lives (Crimean War, Boxer Rebellion, Spanish-American War, Korea, and so on) and there is a chance that a group of well-armored, heavily armed bloodsuckers will be ripping fully automatic fire and maybe mortars and RPGs at you. Or you might just get some vampires with hunting rifles. Depending on how heavy the return fire is, either hold your ground and pour it on them, or get the hell out of there.

Random Question: Are there any non-physical forms of vampire torture, such as forcing them to listen to extremely loud music or depriving them of sleep?

Vampires are very good at turning inward, into something like a deep meditative state, and ignoring all outside stimulus. Knocking them on the head to keep them awake won't be particularly effective. And subjecting them to endless reruns of the Jerry Lewis Telethon or current episodes of *The View* won't make a vampire start babbling away all its vampiric secrets. The only thing that works to somewhat control a vampire is the threat of starvation.

Vampire attack: Some covens—usually those with a large and powerful membership—will have a significant number of vampires under orders to fight back, regardless of the risk to themselves. Think of the Uruk-hai in *The Lord of the Rings*, and you've got a bit of a picture. These vampires will be smeared with tar or some other thick, opaque skin covering to protect against the sun, and will be armored and armed. Regardless of what implements they will or won't have, they're going to be coming at you full tilt. With enough people on your side, you might be able to quickly dispatch a small number of these—about ten, perhaps. More than that and there's going to be mayhem ("mayhem" in its original sense—the loss of limbs; not, "Oh, dude, everything's so crazy right now"). But if you have the extraordinarily bad luck of attacking a coven that has somehow attracted a great number of members and secured them well in a large building or warehouse, you might just witness a full-on vampire charge. If you live to tell, you most likely won't be able to talk about it.

Coven-busting is tough business, and when you think about everything that you really need to tend to—keeping the house secure, guarding family and friends, and trying to keep your body and mind together—going after covens is tilting at vampire-filled windmills. Only when you reach a great deal of community consensus that the vampires in your area have created a coven and that destroying it is sensible should you attempt any of the above tasks, assuming that you can't get in touch with military forces and tip them off to its location. Sure, there's always the risk of a bomb or artillery shell going wide, but hopefully the dogfaces and grunts will facilitate a "surgical strike."

There Is No Overkill: Obliterate, Decapitate, Cremate

Remember that scene from *Donnie Brasco* when the undercover cop has to help kill and cut up a bunch of mobsters? You might want to watch it again, just to get a sense of the unpleasantness of victory against the undead. Even regular readers of *Fangoria* are going to taste their chili dogs in the backs of their throats when they get down to the real nitty-gritty business of sawing and burning bunches of bloodsuckers. It will take quite a bit of mental toughness at first—perhaps try convincing yourself you're processing green-tofu mannequins, and it'll go OK.

Yeah, green tofu—smells good.

Aim for "Center Mass"

This is a principal taught in most shooting courses, including those for police officers. Few people are quick enough to make good head shots under combat speed and stress, so go for the biggest target: the chest. Sure, if you can or must shoot a leech in the head, go for it—but don't waste more ammo on undead running around the house like decapitated

Practice makes perfect

chickens, just trip them. Otherwise, knock big holes in the vampire chests with your shotgun, and you will succeed.

For Sure: Cut the Head Off

When the shooting has ended and the vampire is dead, decapitate it as a final flourish.Use your axe. Do your hacking in the bathtub, or over a cement trough, or some other container that will catch the vampire blood. (Vampires that are lying dead outside can be brought in with a meat hook on a pole or rope, but have your shooter team provide cover for this operation.)Then bag the head in a plastic garbage bag and stash it and the body in a closet or trunk until morning. Don't leave it out where other vampires can see it through a window, although they will be able to smell vampire blood in the air. Sop up the blood with peroxide or bleach, and clean the mop with hot water or bleach (pretend you finally got that job as an RN if you start gagging).

Burn Hot and Long

The key to burning a vampire corpse is firing it thoroughly and long enough. This requires a lot of heat, because burning bodies is not easy. Modern crematoriums burn human cadavers at roughly 1,700° Fahrenheit. You won't be able to get close to that in a fire in the backyard unless you somehow incorporate a propane burner. Otherwise, you'll have to generate as hot a fire as you can using a good bit of wood and charcoal, and sometimes gasoline (but be aware of its volatility).

Using rebar or other metal spars, create a pyre large enough for two or three vampire bodies. You want to make a pyre rather than a fire pit because it allows air to circulate under the bodies, accelerating the burning. If you can find a way to rig a propane system under this, you might have yourself a patentable product and a new business. Build a base layer of kindling, starter logs, and larger pieces of wood. Get a strong fire going first, and then add your dead vampires. Put in your bloodsucker's body and its head, and then add more wood until you've got a bit of a pile. You're going to need about eighty pounds of wood per bloodsucker to have sufficient cremation.

You might also want to dismember a vampire before cremation. This allows for arrangement of the parts in such a way as to facilitate burning. You can layer arms and legs with the wood to burn them completely. Torsos and heads don't burn easily or quickly.

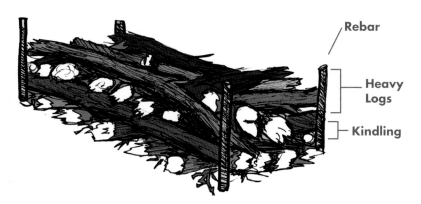

Rebar

Heavy Logs

Kindling

Vampire Fact:

The ghoul has long been associated with the vampire and vampirism, but by definition, the relatively mindless ghoul eats the actual flesh (muscle tissue, etc.) of the living, whereas the much more intelligent vampire seeks nothing but blood (which is also a tissue). The origins of the ghoul are found in Arabic folklore: The *ghul* or *ghulah* (male and female, respectively) was a demonic spirit that inhabited burial sites and ate the flesh of the dead. Appropriations of the ghoul in modern film and literature made this creature an undead, reanimated human cannibal, with little of the cachet, organization, and lineage of the vampire.

This sounds quite involved. Well, it is. *You're not making s'mores*—you're trying to burn very tough flesh and bone down to cinders. If you're in the undertaking business, you will be smart to subcontract with a vampire-corpse pickup service, as the government will probably contract you to run your crematorium steadily to get rid of the undead. Yes, you can probably invest in that condo in Belize *now*, 'cause a vampire uprising is an undertaker's windfall.

Disposing of Final Remains

If you build a perfect fire, you'll reduce your vampire to ashes and major bones—skull, ribs, spine, pelvis, humeri, and femurs. Smash these and bury them. Don't leave bones lying around, and don't do some weird thing like hang vampire skeletons from trees or decorate your mailbox with a skull—that's just unsightly and you never know who might notice and take a disliking. At the end of the epidemic, when vampire counts in your area have reached near zero, you can dismantle or hide the pyre for future use.

Photographing and Filming Dead Vampires

In the hunting and fishing business, there's something known as the "grip 'n' grin": a photo of an angler or hunter posing with his quarry. The deer hunter holding up the head of a whitetail buck by its antlers. A fisherman holding aloft a gut-bucket bass by its lower jaw. A kid with a .44-caliber revolver posing next to a huge feral hog he shot a dozen times.

There will be a temptation among many citizens to do the same with vampires—to pose with shot-dead undead, smile big, and snap photos. Many people will also videotape their success at blowing holes in vampires, and surely numerous videos will be made of bonfires of dead vampires. YouTube will probably have to add on about 10,000 TB to accommodate all the home videos of shooting, killing, posing, and burning vampires, and even little skits and plays using vampire bodies.

Taking photos of vampires you kill to have a record of what happened—for insurance purposes, historical rea-

Random Question: Is it bad karma if I keep vampire trophies, like ears or hands, or a skull?

You probably don't want to hang on to any vampire parts. First, every vampire used to be someone, and if it turns out you have the body part of someone's relative, you might have a problem. Second, if other vampires find out you have a body part, they might get a little pissed off.

Everyone wants some kind of trophy or souvenir of strange and difficult passages in life, but maybe pick something that doesn't come from a vampire, like, say, the last shell from your gun on the night of your biggest shootout, or a memento from a friend who died, or get a tattoo. Anything derived from a vampire body poses risks.

sons, and as a sheer document—is a legit idea. Acting silly with vampire bodies, however, casts you in a bad light. Propping up dead vampires in a chair holding a can of Bud, putting Mickey Mouse ears on dead vampires, or taking shooter-team trophy shots with everyone gathered round the deceased leech flashing pseudo gang signs are all bad ideas. You don't want a record of that to get back to other vampires. Photograph dead vampires alone, with no one else in the photo.

You also don't want to post videos on YouTube of your drunk mother dancing with a dead vampire in the living room, or of you hosting some kind of creepy, fake talk show with a bunch of dead vampires in chairs and you as moderator. Same reason: You're putting out a statement that can turn you into a target.

Sometimes in life, you stumble upon trouble, and that can't be helped. Sometimes you make trouble when you don't have to. *So don't.*

Proper Handling of Dead Vampires

Anything dead should be regarded as toxic to one degree or another. Human blood is a major component of toxic hospital waste. And with vampires coming at you in physical states varying from mildly blemished, athletic glamour to partially suppurated freaks, you can't put too much of a premium on cleanliness (can we ever, really?).

Toxicity of Dead Vampires

Vampires can host innumerable viruses and bacteria without ever suffering any ailment, but they can pass

Vampire Fact:

The Kashubian people, of northeastern Poland, identify two different kinds of vampires at birth. The *vjesci* was born with a caul over its face. If this caul was not kept, dried, ground into a potion, and given to the child on his or her seventh birthday, the child would eventually turn into a vampire. The other newborn bloodsucker was the *wupji*, a baby born with two visible teeth. This tot was a natural-born vampire and could not be cured in any way. To destroy a vampire, the Kashubians would decapitate a bloodsucker and put the severed head between its feet, similar to the Serbian practice.

on those pathogens to humans through direct contact. The Centers for Disease Control is extremely concerned about vampires spreading flu, meningitis, varieties of herpes, and, startlingly, the bubonic plague. So protect yourself accordingly.

Protective Clothing for Vampire Disposal

Killing vampires will be messy business, and having to move a shotgunned bloodsucker can expose a person to contaminated blood and viscera. For this reason, wear thick gloves and eye protection when moving a vampire body, and touch it as little as possible. Using a cart or simply dragging a dead vampire by meat hook is the best way to go. If you have the means, bag the vampire with supersize garbage bags before moving it.

Vampire Fact:
Three notable vampire-like entities from Hinduism are the *rakshasas, vetalas,* and *bhutas*. The demonic *rakshasas* wander at night, have long fangs, and attack infants and pregnant women. *Vetalas* are spirits that take over and reanimate dead humans, while the *bhutas* can enter and possess a living person, although neither of these two demons do much in the way of actually drinking blood. The goddess of destruction, Kali, is known for a massive bloodthirstiness, among other horrendous attributes, and the Hindu god of death, Yama, often depicted with fangs and smeared blood, attacks the wandering spirits of the dead who committed wrongdoing in life.

Proper Disposal Location

If you're smart, you've probably sealed off the cellar (see chapter 4), so you can't drop bodies there. Pick a closet or back room that isn't used often and stash the leech there temporarily, bagged or covered, and mark the door so that no one enters the room. In the daylight, burn the body properly. If you're unable to make a fire, dispose of the body in a dump after decapitating it. In the sun, dead vampires burn quite a bit more slowly than live ones, but they do eventually roast down to just bones after a week or so. Vultures and other scavengers do not eat vampire flesh.

Dealing with a Mess o' Dead Vampires

Let's say you live in a town with a lot of vampires and you've had a heck of a night sitting on your roof with your ArmaLite. Now you've got thirty dead vampires lying all around. While this is unlikely, there will be those dedicated citizens who, very well armed, will do just so.

Prepare for this scenario ahead of time by doing two things. First, build a pyre big enough to hold at least five vampires at once. If you're killing this many vampires, you've probably burned a few before and know how much wood is necessary for a complete burn. Second, rig up a bunch of meat hooks on poles so you can just drag the undead to the fire rather than touch them. Towing them with an ATV or riding mower works fine, too.

Start cremations in the morning so you've got enough time to roast the bodies all day. Think of it as a cross between a pep rally and heavy-duty religious service, and the time will go by pleasantly.

One note: You should keep a log of the vampires you kill, recording identifying marks or clothing, and the spot where you bury or dispose of the final remains (bones). This is mainly for your own knowledge and personal history. While some people will crow about how many vampires they killed, the better bet is to admit to some mildly successful shooting and leave it at that.

Vampire Fact:

Cashing in on the unbeatable combination of alcohol and vampirism (and as a reflection of red wine as a blood metaphor) American importers twice offered a "vampire wine" in the 1990s. The first was an Italian red wine in a black bottle that came in a coffin-shaped box; the second was a Romanian wine. The Austrian distiller Stroh capitalized on the 1993 opening of the film *Bram Stoker's Dracula* in Bucharest, Romania, by simultaneously marketing a fruit-flavored, red-colored vodka called "Dracula's Spirit." A "Dracula Slivovitz" appeared in 1994.

Only You Can Prevent Vampire Reanimation

If you think that reanimation is not a problem, consider that nearly every vampire coven—those known to American intelligence services as well as many unknown—has a team of vampires trained in reanimation methods and a handy supply of blood dedicated to such endeavors. It's not easy, and not always successful, but many vampires that had "bled out" have been recovered, their wounds sewn, and their veins pumped full of vampire blood. This is no longer something that only the most powerful or important vampires can enjoy. The spread of the know-how and technology will result in many vampire reanimations during the coming period of attack. So follow a few rules:

Don't Let Them Get Away

"It's only a flesh wound" can't be exaggerated with vampires. Often, even the loss of a limb is not a life-threatening wound for a vampire. If you wing a vampire with some buckshot, shoot again. If you're shooting at a vampire with a pistol or carbine, shoot several times for the center mass. Your shooter team, and you, should practice follow-up shots in case you hit a vampire that's halfway in a door, or hit one while it's outside, and it starts to run. Are tracer bullets worthwhile? (These are bullets with a pyrotechnic insert that lights up and glows so that the shooter can track the direction of the shot.) Only in situations where you're using a carbine or rifle and trying to hit a distant target, such as if you go outside with your team at night and try to zap a vampire across the road or in a nearby field. If you're facing a multi-vampire attack, or a lot of leeches are moving through your neighborhood, tracers might not be a bad idea with an assault rifle or carbine (load one for every three rounds).

Don't Let Them Pile Up

If you've got three or more vampire bodies, make some fire. Don't stockpile more than five bodies before you perform cremations. Bodies are difficult to burn entirely, and the more of them you've got piled up, the bigger a pyre you're going to have to build and the more fuel you'll need. Unless you have access to a very good furnace, don't leave the leeches around to molder.

Vampire Fact:

In a blood-drenched narrative covering everything from animal sacrifice to issues about menstruation, the book of Leviticus states clearly what must be the earliest Judeo-Christian proscription against human vampirism, as Jehovah instructs Moses to tell the Israelites, "If any Israelite or alien settled in Israel consumes any blood, I shall set my face against him and cut him off from his people, because the life of a creature is the blood, and I appoint it to make expiation on the altar for yourselves: it is the blood, which is life, that makes expiation. . . . Any Israelite or alien settled in Israel who hunts beasts or birds that may lawfully be eaten must drain out the blood and cover it with earth, because the life of every living creature is its blood" (Lev. 17:10–14).

Addressing Neighbors with Too Many Dead Vampires on Their Lawn

Most townships and boroughs have ordinances about eye-sores on private property. But with the breakdown of social order that will come with the widespread vampire attack, local ordinance enforcement might take a backseat to survival. Suddenly, you might notice that your neighbor across the way has undead piled in the front yard like spilled cordwood. This will cause some problems.

One, it will stink. Two, it will attract other vampires in droves, intent on killing the vampire killer inside the house. In suburban legal parlance, this might be termed an "attractive nuisance."

So how do you politely encourage disposal? Well, you might call up your neighbor and say, "Hey, Zeke, how's it going? Listen, man, the neighborhood is so totally thrilled you've shot so many bloodsuckers. You *da man*. You need any help getting rid of them? It's going to be dark soon."

If your neighbor is tired, or just plain uninterested, you might have to wait a bit. But if nothing gets done, you should gather a few other neighbors, knock on his door, and offer to help. Some people are just lazy, some are really messy, and some really like to gaze out the front window at a yard full of dead vampires (in this case, you might want to bring in mental-health services). One way or another, though, those bodies need to be burned.

Random Question: I'd really like to try my hand at vampire reanimation. Does anyone make a starter kit, like, say Novo Nordisk or DeWalt?

Listen, you don't want to get into vampire reanimation, not even for kicks. Sure, everyone wants to try it once, but if you pull it off, then what have you got? A raving, ravenous, lunatic vampire that's going to suck dry the first thing it can find: you. Of course, the Department of Defense is going to be picking up dead vampires and warehousing them by the ton in the hopes of creating an invincible vampire army, so . . .

OK fine, here's how you do it:

Materials:

- One fully intact, dead (blood-empty) vampire that doesn't have too many holes, most likely one that starved or bled to death less than two weeks ago. (Dead vampires tend to turn an ugly jaundiced or putty color, their eyes grow colorless and glazed, and their bodies appear deflated.)
- Three or four transfusion kits.
- Six pints of human or animal blood and ten pints of vampire blood (good luck getting that).
- A military field-surgery kit.
- Chains and shackles.
- Your favorite shotgun (as if you wouldn't have it with you).

Procedures:

Chain the vampire to a table as securely as possible. Don't use rope, as vampires can claw through it. Elevate the vampire's feet just a bit.

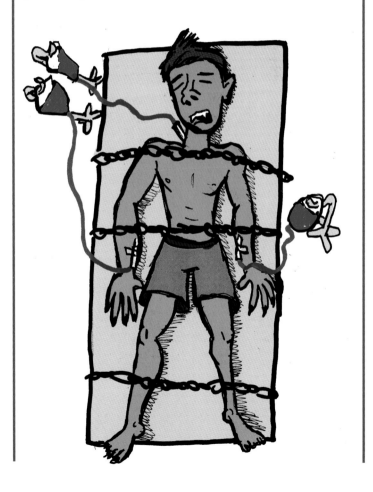

Insert the transfusion needles into veins on both arms and put two into the jugular vein. That's not easy to pierce.

First transfuse two or three pints of vampire blood, depending upon how big the vampire is. For a vampire over 250 pounds, start with seven pints of vampire blood. Next, transfuse all of the human blood, and then follow that with the remaining vampire blood. Do this as quickly as possible—the vampire body should readily absorb the transfusions.

The vampire should show signs of life after forty-eight hours, probably sooner. Blood will begin to occlude the eyeballs and surface veins, and varicosities will begin to turn blue, purple, and red again. The vampire will also try to move and will eventually regain complete consciousness and take a very strong disliking to you.

And that's when you'll have to shoot it.

Chapter 4

Saving Your Own Neck (and a Few Others)

During vampire uprisings, the bloodsuckers hunt in all places—sleepy small towns, tony beach communities, cities small and large, and your nice upstate weekend home. At times of significant activity you can expect repeated nightly visitations for weeks or more, as you'll be at home because of local or regional curfews (the people with the badges, guns, and law degrees are going to be enforcing all sorts of security measures, and your Libertarian nerves will be frayed). So you might spend a bit of your time fortifying the homestead: barring windows, securing doors, and closing off spaces you can't always control, like attics. Daylight hours will give you time to assess your property and look for signs of attempted entry or other vampire activity, such as footprints, marks on windows, and vampire graffiti.

Home Defenses

Vampires are capable of terrific physical feats. They can come through small openings—even openings that seem too small for a person. They often have terrific strength and can break and lift things people can't. But they're not bulldozers. They can't come crashing through well-built walls or pull back the roof.

But there's no sense giving them any chance to squirm or shove their way in. When vampire-proofing your house, think as if you're trying to keep out both rats and bears, and you'll do all right.

Sealing Unnecessary Entryways

Certainly, you're going to want to get in and out of your house easily enough during daylight hours. You want to hang on to your social life, don't you?

So, pick three ways in and out (including your escape door): two on the main floor, and one on an upper level, if you have more than one story. Put extra dead bolts on these doors. Seal off any other entrances: patio doors, side doors, and the odd porch door. Simply bar these with 2 x 4s and nails or screws.

Sliding glass doors present a particular problem. Burglars love them, and vampires will, too, especially given their terrific talent for quietly and quickly cutting glass. You're going to have to somehow bar these with metal or wood beams that you can secure to the door frame or walls and floor with brackets. Not easy, but do it, because otherwise sliding glass is just a big gaping hole. You also need to jam the slide.

Cutting Off Attics and Cellars

Your upper-level escape door can be in the attic, but bear in mind that once you retreat to the attic, that's where you're stuck, and if there's a way out through a vent or eave, you're going to be at least two stories up once you're on the roof. Think you and your kids can jump that far,

Chevy Chase? And given that you can't always control who or what gets on the roof, sealing off the attic is the way to go. Bar that door.

As for the cellar, you would best avoid that as a retreat and location of an escape door (see later in this chapter for a discussion of escape routes). You don't want to get stuck underground with vampires above you and with your means of escape upstairs on ground level. You want to be able to see your surroundings before you escape, and most likely you won't have any view of the outside when you try to emerge from cellar doors or windows. If you encounter vampires going out a ground-level door, you're on their level and can blast them. Coming out of a cellar, you're looking at their feet. *Not good.* Bar the cellar doors.

One caveat: If you happen to live in one of those homes that has a cellar with secret passageways that leads to outer houses or to the river where they used to take shipments of rum during Prohibition, you might be pretty freakin' lucky. This, indeed, could be a primo escape route. Bear in mind that the vampires will likely find the other end of the passageway, though. If you decide to leave your home via this underground tunnel, go with the understanding that you are going to be shooting your way to the other end. Frequently monitor this passageway during your extended stay in your home. Do this during the day when vampires are mostly inactive, but remember it'll be dark in there and the leeches can function fully, so spotlight and shoot. If you find the passage is simply too lousy with the undead, burn them out, shoot them, then seal it off—it's too risky.

Securing Windows

From the first major literary vampire work in English, *Varney the Vampire, or The Feast of Blood*, to every *Dracula* movie, one thing has been made clear: The undead can slip through a window like mist. This, in fact, is one source of the myths about vampires shape-shifting into animals (bats, snakes, butterflies) or substances (gases, fluids): They seem to get in through the tiniest cracks.

Not exactly. Among the numerous survival skills the undead acquire is a magician's ability to cut glass with honed fingernails or self-made tools. They can remove panes of class so quickly and neatly that the pane appears to have simply fallen loose.

The solution is simple: Bar windows with metal shanks or wrought-iron shafts, securing them to the wall or top and bottom of the sill with at least three-fourths-inch screws. You still want to be able to see out the window, so don't cover it entirely, and you still want to be able to open it (usually, to be able to shoot a vampire outside), so attach the bars to the wall. You want to be sure that there is no space between the bars wider than a child's body, moving sideways, because of course there are going to be kiddie vampires—didn't you see that girl from *Spider-Man* in *Interview with the Vampire*?

Next, screw brackets into the window frame and jam, locking the window in place. You can remove these when necessary to open the window when on watch or when shooting at vampires. When the weather is warm, you can bracket the window in place with *no more than an inch* of space at the bottom for airflow, and only on second-story windows.

Do not bar windows with sections of wood. A vampire can cut the glass, reach in, and break the wood or tear it off the window.

Where do you get metal spars or wrought-iron shafts? Junkyards, dumps, Pottery Barn, or abandoned houses, or you can take parts from cars and mountain bikes. Tear apart that stupid lawn sculpture you've been screwing with for six years and use that.

Securing Operating Doors

You have to be able to get in and out of your home during the day. At night, however, secure the main door using three or four 2 x 10 studs mounted in securable collars bolted to the wall or door frame. Consider adding a small sliding peephole to the door to allow you to look out and shoot at approaching vampires.

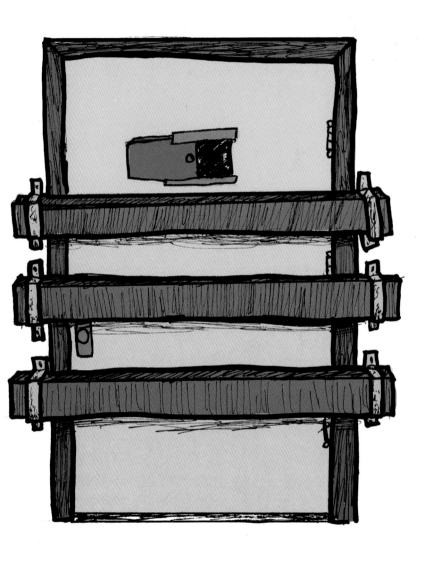

Outside the House

Should you put vampire deterrents on the outside of your house? Such things might give you, the homeowner, peace of mind when taking on human criminals. ("Ah, yes, that prowler is going to slide right off the deck with all that silicon grease I spread out there.") But such things as barbed wire, concertina wire, and spiked boards don't work against vampires that ignore superficial wounds and can deftly cross physical barriers. You might get the idea to wrap electrified livestock fencing around your home, but that would work only if vampires were as docile as cows. The undead will simply cut the wire, and that will be that.

Warning Systems

Although vampire deterrents generally don't work, there are a few low-tech things you can put in place to help herald the arrival of the undead.

A dog: Dogs really hate vampires, and vampires really hate dogs. You don't need a big dog, just one that's not afraid to bark when there's an undead UPS guy coming up the walk. Dogs are loathe to do physical battle with vampires (dogs are smart enough to know when the odds are really crappy), so there's little sense in getting some big attack dog that will need a lot of food. What's the perfect dog? The dog from *Mad Max 2: The Road Warrior*, whose name was, simply, Dog. A blue heeler, he was medium-sized and didn't eat much; he was quick, he was cunning, he took orders, he was loyal, and he only opened his mouth when he needed to.

Bells, chimes, or beer cans: Some bloodsuckers were tango champions in their human life (it's true) and can move like a breeze. Others were stevedores and beer-truck drivers and are klutzes. And despite their senses and abilities, the newly undead are still getting down the routine. You can set simple, small alarms for these latter types: a cluster of reindeer bells hung from a window or door that will drop to the floor if jarred; a stack of pebble-filled beer cans at the bottom edge of the cellar door; a very light thread running along the floor, connected to a chime on the ceiling. These might sound silly, but they can work, and you're going to have time on your hands, as night-time entertainment is going to be a bit of a stretch.

Sand or dirt patches outside: During the day, you can go outside safely, although don't do so alone or while groggy. Go armed, alert, and with a partner. While outside, spread sand or fine dirt in front of the entrances and at other various places around the house. Make this deep enough that it forms a solid surface, with no grass poking through, and rake it clean every day. Check it in the mornings for footprints. Experienced vampires will go around it. New and inept ones won't. And you'll also find out what humans might be roving around, looking for a place to stay or for stuff to steal.

Random Question: Should I leave the city for my country home, or should I stay in the penthouse?

Jeez, life is full of hard choices, isn't it?

How remote is your country home? Is it really far away from anything else? If so, the isolation might make it too dangerous a proposition. Plus, there's all the upkeep that will distract you, and the damn deer keep eating the bushes and you get so angry at them your blood pressure goes up and you start drinking, and suddenly you're shooting at pictures of your parents and you run out of ammo, and then you see a pale greenish face at the window . . .

Of course, a penthouse will be a target, as vampires are highly attracted to upper stories that might be easily penetrated. How secure can you make the penthouse? Also, who is going to be there with you? You might offer sanctuary to a bunch of really fun friends and you can party all through these nights of danger. Think about it: How many people will be able to say they got lucky in a penthouse while the vampire uprisings raged?

Yeah, stay in the city.

Locking Up at Night

The easiest way to do this is to work up a checklist of every door and window, listing every dead bolt, inside bolt, and window lock. Run through the list prior to sundown, ticking off every locking point, and then pick your lookout spots for the night and hunker down. Have two complete master sets of keys and make sure they're kept on your person and someone else's person, not left in the "key bowl" in the kitchen. If you're alone, have one set of keys on you, and very carefully hide the other set.

What If the Power Goes Off?

In most places, utility service will remain intact, but there might be drops in power or in the delivery of fuels, owing to personnel issues (employees not reporting for work but tending to the security of their families) or security issues (vampires attacking generating stations or service centers). In places where a group of vampires intends to target an isolated neighborhood, they cut power cables. And economic insecurities might cause utility companies to cut back on production or insist customers cut consumption.

Simply assume that at some point, in each season, warm or cold, you will loose electricity and heat. Prepare for this. Keep fuel tanks as full as possible, which will be a financial liability if your vampire-fighting necessitates time off from

Vampire Fact:
The Greeks were probably the first people in Western civilization to identify bloodsucking entities, calling them the *lamiai*. Unlike modern vampires, which are actual, corporeal beings, the *lamiai* were spirit beings that could transform into beautiful women to seduce and drink the blood of young men. But just like current vampires, they could multiply their own ranks.

work, or wide-spread uprisings across entire regions disrupt the economy, leading to lay-offs. Batteries, kerosene heaters, gas-powered generators, and camping lanterns are all good things to have.

Few people know how to repair high-tension lines if these are damaged and you are without power. In this sense, you're at the mercy of the power company's ability to respond to utility issues of vampire uprisings. Who knows how good that will be? Practice taking cold showers now.

Escape Routes

Leaving your domicile is the last thing that you want to do. Seriously, stay put in your place for as long as you can. Even if you've got dead vampires all over the place, don't leave. Yes, they stink like old casserole, but don't leave.

The only two circumstances in which you might have to leave are if the home has sustained so much damage that it's no longer viable (this might include being on fire), or so many vampires have entered your house that you cannot kill them all, and you're overwhelmed.

If you're going on foot (not the best choice) map out an escape route ahead of time. Pick the specific egress—upper floor window, side door—and have a predetermined destination that is not too far away and in a roughly direct

course from your home. With luck, this is another structure on your property, or a neighbor's house or apartment. Practice this run several times.

This is a last-ditch, desperate maneuver, and if you're doing
it because so many vampires have arrived at your house,
your chances are slim once you're outside. Seriously, how
fast can you run? How many kids do you have? How slow
is your spouse?

The best form of escape is in a vehicle, the bigger the better
(how American). This is where all you Hummer owners get
to do your little happy dance. A big vehicle has two distinct
advantages: One, you can stock it with supplies and ammo,
pre-escape, and still have room for the spouse and kids (this is
assuming you're not going to take advantage of this crisis to
run off and start a new life in Amsterdam). Two, you can run
over some damn vampires. You can't do that in a Mini Cooper.
Again, map out your escape route. Know where you're going once you're flying down the street. While driving around
and running down vampires sounds like fun, you'll be wast-
ing precious gasoline, and if you bog down or crash, you're
a sitting duck. Get to your escape-route destination ASAP,
don't waste time or gas, and when you arrive, quickly set up
a home defense or join someone else's.

For those of you who just couldn't hold back and bought the
Mini Cooper, you've got enough room in that thing for about
four hours of supplies, and you're going to have to drive

around the vampires. Bear in mind that all it takes is one strong vampire, or five fifth-grader vampires, to flip a Mini.

Defending Against a Multivampire Attack

Although it's rare, at some point, your home might be targeted by a group of vampires or an entire coven. This is very bad, but not impossible to fight off. Covens do sometimes go on the attack, but usually only in cases in which the bloodsuckers believe they need strength in numbers because they are attacking a structure occupied by a number of capable humans. Their actual reasons will be unknown to you, but most likely they suspect that there are a few able-bodied, armed members of the home, or the home is beset by illness, or the structure is simply secured poorly. Of course, some vampires have fetishes for certain kinds of people: plus-sized models past their prime, or obese, cherubic young men. Vampires who share such proclivities will sometimes gang up and hunt down the sexy-fat objects of their sanguine desires. Keep in mind that covens will have their own spotters and spies, and vampires could have your home under surveillance all night for weeks without making a move. Regardless of how many people you have in your household, you must drill for this. Maybe it's just you and your affectionate but inept husband. Maybe it's you and four friends you met through Craigslist. Whatever the case, you're going to have to work up a set of plans to counter a multiple-vampire attack.

Vampire Fact:

The first European female vampire (or vampire-like woman) of note was Hungarian countess Elizabeth Bathory, who through the late 1500s and into the early 1600s tortured and, legend has it, bathed in the blood of 650 youth, mostly virginal women. Such baths were supposed to preserve her beauty. While no evidence of actual blood bathing was presented at her trial in 1611, her own handwritten tally of her victims, by name, brought her conviction and solitary confinement. She died in prison in 1614, most likely a serial killer, although she has often been referred to as "the female Dracula."

Single-person resistance: Let's spot you one advantage—say, you've actually secured the house quite well. On a multi-floor house, stay on the ground floor and, if possible, seal off the upper floors. Under attack, shoot the bloodsuckers as best you can, as they force their way through secured windows, doors, and weak structural spots. When you realize that one is about to get in and has others behind it, grab your crash bag and tactical vest and head for your escape route. Barricading yourself in a room isn't a workable idea. While you might be able to run to a corner room and secure the door sufficiently behind you, if the leeches really want you, they're going to make short work of that door, using axes or something heavier. They might decide one person isn't worth the work, but if you present a blood feast of such enticement to them (you're diabetic but otherwise a healthy, attractive, 220-pound former cheerleader *and* a virgin), they're coming through that door and you can't operate a shotgun fast enough to get all of them. "Her blood tastes like Cool Whip," is the compliment you won't live to hear.

Couples and three-person resistance: Again, stay on the ground floor and seal off the upper floors, if possible. Keep open boxes of ammo in easily accessible areas and a quantity in your vest or pockets (Orvis makes a lovely shotgun-shell carrying pouch). Assign each person a section of the ground floor to defend. Doubly secure everything if possible, psyche yourselves up (seriously, get mad), and exercise as much fire discipline as you can: "One shot, one kill," as they say. If a vampire is getting in, call out the location. The closest shooter comes to your help. Don't let a live vampire get too far into the house. Kill it, and return to your post. If someone loses their nerve and calls out for the escape route, settle them down. At least two people (or both members of the couple) need to call for an escape before you take off. Once you start down that route, stick to the previously determined travel plan and destination.

Four to eight people: Be sure you've chosen one person to be completely in charge, and then a number two. These are the people who will decide, together, to make an escape attempt if necessary. Assign each person a window, door, or staircase (assuming you feel you can keep an upper floor open), and enforce strict fire discipline—more people means more shooting means you run out of shotgun shells a lot faster and also stand a better chance of accidentally shooting one of your own.

Twelve people or more: You might call this your "Vampire Killin' Hoedown." Assuming each member of your dozen-, fifteen-, or twenty-five-member extended family has a firearm, knows how to use it, and is highly motivated, you are going to start cleaning up. Build a shooting tower (or two) as soon as you can and use it frequently. Such a tower is similar to a forest-fire watchtower, but nowhere near as tall. Let the leeches know they're always going to take fire from there. You might put an AR-15 or M1A up there, too, and let 'er rip now and then. If you've never seen an exploding vampire lit up by tracer rounds in the dark, you're in for a treat. Vampires will come to think of your house as a source of serious trouble, and, in a way similar to gang warfare, you might face a mini-invasion—scores of vampires that lay siege to your house, using various implements of destruction, such as battering rams, wire cutters, plastic explosives, and armored vehicles. But a well-fortified structure effectively defended can withstand a lot. Keeping your own head, and keeping your family focused, will be the greater task. With that many vampires outside, there's little use for an escape route above ground. It's Alamo time.

Potential Disasters

A complete plan of home defense wouldn't be complete without "thinking about the unthinkable"—the absolute worst that could happen, which often involves multiple bloodsuckers and/or the destruction of the domicile. Before you get into these kinds of situations, you have to know already if you're willing to sacrifice yourself to attempt to save family members or friends, or if you will make the necessary moves to save yourself when you realize that all bets are off.

The following examples were taken from recent but isolated vampire uprisings, precursors of things to come:

Entire family trapped in one room: A family of six in rural western Arkansas was found all together, drained of blood, in a single back room. Multiple vampires had forced their way in, cutting off any escape route, and the family re-treated. The bloodsuckers attacked the room from inside the house and through the windows until the family ran out of limited ammunition and then died at the hands of the vampires. One family member suffered an accidental gunshot wound in the back during the mayhem. *Lesson:* Under multiple-vampire attack, post a guard on the exit to the escape route and position any nonfighting family members nearby. Carry at least a dozen rounds of ammunition in addition to what you load in your firearm.

House on fire, multiple vampires outside: In the burned heap of a house in suburban southern New Jersey, the bodies of eight members of an extended family were found in the basement where they had died of smoke inhalation, not vampire attack. *Lesson:* If you cannot extinguish a fire in the house, escape the structure; don't try to survive the fire in the basement. Head out with enough ammo and shoot your way to safety.

Vampire Fact:

In times when *Blutsaugers* were on the loose at night, Bavarian officials gave out one of the most specific instructions in all of vampire lore about using animals as guards against the undead: Residents who had large black dogs were told to paint big bright eyes on the animals' heads. The *Blutsauger* would see the dog from a distance, believe the dog (asleep or not) was on the lookout, and avoid the house. Residents were also told to spread hawthorn around their homes, rub raw garlic cloves around doors and windows, and then stay put all night.

Vampires entering from multiple points, family scattered in home: Near Gainesville, Florida, five single friends died separately from one another in a large suburban home. Evidence in the house indicated that several vampires had entered from the basement, and the friends scattered in panic. Two of them, young men, attempted to fight the vampires using knives, and failed. *Lesson:* Discipline your team members to stick together and fight together. Nonfighting members should remain together in a given place.

Running out of ammunition: On the Maine coast, the off-season crew of four at a resort compound disappeared. Investigators found two empty shotguns, eight spent shells, and one empty ammunition box. Blast marks on the walls indicated that the crew missed all of their shots but two, causing no real damage, but spattering blood that tested positive as vampire blood. *Lesson:* Use an ammunition belt or shotgun-shell pouch, and stockpile as much ammo as you can.

Escape route or secondary shelter fails: This is probably checkmate, as a family of six on the shores of Lake Ontario learned horribly. Their scattered, headless, bloodless bodies indicated they had fled their house but ran into some seriously vicious vampires on their way to a neighbor's barn. Several family members were armed, but they apparently fired few rounds outside, suggesting that they were flushed into a trap and had little time to fight back. The house had only one sign of forced entry—a broken window frame, suggesting that only one or two bloodsuckers entered the house. *Lesson:* Fight in the house as fiercely as possible before you abandon the domicile, and be willing to face down a half a dozen vampires at once. Practice the escape route in the daylight, and know exactly how to get to the secondary shelter, which should be fortified. Take your spotlights and flashlights with you and illuminate your way as you go; the vampires know you've run out, so you might as was well light them up to shoot them.

Trapping Vampires

There are few trap configurations that most people can build or purchase that will hold a vampire in place. Most bloodsuckers are often too cunning to get nabbed, and too strong to be held by wire snares.

The main point of an effective trap is to hold a vampire in place long enough for you to get a shotgun bead on it. So you'll be setting traps close to your house or as part of an outdoors ambush close to a secure location. The only time you might venture into farmland or in the woods is to set up an ambush exploiting either a steel-jawed trap or pit trap.

Mechanical Traps

The only mechanical trap most people can deploy effectively against vampires is a commercial wolf trap. These are

Random Question: What are my liabilities if I set a vampire trap and my doofus neighbor blunders into it and gets severely injured or dies?

Given that you probably don't have any kind of protective association with a doofus (for example, you agree to let each other have access to either person's property for anti-vampire efforts), he had no reason to be on your land. There might be a lot of bloodsucking chaos going on, but that's no reason for people not to observe property rights. Many states have laws that protect property owners from the misadventures of trespassers. Plus, given that many of the anti-vampire efforts that will be undertaken by citizens during an uprising will have no legal precedent or interpretation of their effects, legally you'll be vulnerable only to a civil suit from your doofus neighbor's family, if they decide to sue. But given his doofusy nature, you might call him before you build the trap and tell him where it is and just to be mindful of it. And then he'll walk down there to look at it and fall in.

heavy and strong and can be anchored well. You can buy decent ones online for about sixty dollars each, and they're not too difficult to use, although they are a tad hazardous. You'll have to learn how to camouflage these completely so that they might work. The advantage to wolf traps is that you will be able to identify whether you have accidentally trapped a person or have actually caught a vampire (people squeal and scream; vampires emit a kind of snarling you will never forget).

Random Question: If I catch a vampire, is keeping him or her as a domestic servant wrong (saying I use all the necessary hardware, like a steel gag, leg irons, and a shock collar)?

With work schedules the way they are these days, what's a busy homemaker to do about the cleaning, the cooking, the kids, and the cremation pyre? A vampire small or weak enough to be captured might seem like it could be quite useful as a domestic servant of some kind, especially one to do some of the dirty jobs, like clean the cat box. But how, exactly, are you going to feed your help? Is your family going to take turns bleeding themselves into a pint glass so your crazed little butler can drink it down?

Your question, however, seems to be an ethical one: Is capturing a strange semi-human creature and forcing it to work in a place it would rather not a decent or reasonable action? No, it's not—it's dangerous to your family, and you will have on your hands a prisoner, not a willing servant. You might encounter a vampire that seeks shelter among humans and is willing to work for its keep (be very suspicious of such a creature), but otherwise, when it comes to domestic servants, stick to illegal human aliens.

There are a couple basic ways to work with these:

Edge of woods or field: Identify a location where vampires appear to travel in and out of your neighborhood along an agricultural field or patch of woods. Set and camouflage the trap just inside the edge of the trees or old cornfield (you need to pick a field that has enough dead corn or winter wheat to hide the shape of the trap in addition to whatever other camouflage you use—leaves, forest litter, etc.). Bait the trap area with fresh blood just before dark and set some sort of object of interest—a bloody briefcase, a broken firearm, or an animal carcass—just beyond the trap. The combination of bloodlust plus a vampire's usual intense curiosity might guide it toward stepping in the trap. Have a three-person shooting team hidden a short distance away, with a clear field of fire to watch with night vision, and then spotlight and shoot the vampire. Again, you'll need a good shotgun, carbine, or rifle. (Don't use a scope with these—just use open sights. By the time the vampire is spotlighted, it will be thrashing its way out of the trap, and you'll waste time trying to keep the crosshairs on it. Line up the sights on the leech's center mass and squeeze the trigger, Hoss.)

Near a secure house or other structure: Camouflage several wolf traps around the house, outside easily accessed shooting positions (shooting from the second floor is best). Keep an eye on these throughout the night, although a trapped vampire will certainly make some commotion. Spotlight, then shoot. And don't forget where you set the traps, or you might have to learn how to resist the vampire horde while hopping around with a broken ankle.

Tiger Pits and Punji Sticks

While this might conjure up images of bad TV movies about the Vietnam War, they can provide some worthwhile assistance in setting up bloodsuckers for your shooter team. But they have some drawbacks, too: They take awhile to make (you need to dig them deep enough), you can't move them, and you need to either be right on top of them to make the shot, or a bit elevated at a short distance. Another problem is their passivity: You can't "turn them off," necessarily, only uncover them during the day so your neighbors can at least see what they're about to land on.

The key to these is to outfit the bottom of the pit with some serious Punji sticks. You need sticks that are about forty inches long and can be set a good twenty-five inches into the ground. The exposed portion should have a very sharp tip with a sizable barb, if possible. You can use several materials to create these: wood, metal, or some kind of polycarbonate. Some machine-shop experience will help with this.

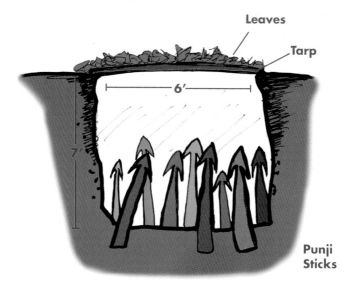

Leaves

Tarp

6'

7'

Punji
Sticks

Make pit traps roughly six feet wide, nine feet long (to take into account bodily motion), and seven feet deep. Set these up in the same locations you would wolf traps—at edges of travel corridors. Cover them with a tarp or camouflage netting that you can obscure with dead leaves and grass. To prevent the cover from sagging, set thin wooden slats along the top of the opening. These will break easily when a vampire or drunk American plunges through.

The three-man team will have to quickly approach the pit once a vampire is inside—two forward (one shining the spotlight, one the shooter), with the third member watching everyone's back. You'll most likely shoot the bloodsucker as it comes out of the pit.

A quick note: You might think that some kind of fire or explosive trap might be effective. They could be, if you have access to a good deal of gel fuel, C-4, and a proper education in demolition. *But who does?* And vampires can smell these chemical substances easily. Fire is going to come into play only when you're burning vampire bodies, or when you have the remote chance of setting fire to a coven's hideout with burning arrows.

Outdoor Self-Defense

If you're stuck outside during a wave of vampires attacks—maybe you lost your home, maybe you're a homeless veteran, or maybe you decided to "get back to the land" at the *really* wrong time—you'd better start channeling some kind of inner being who is a combination of a Sioux warrior, Mad Max, and Mr. T. 'Cause this ain't going to be no damn weenie roast, that's for sure.

Build a shelter: That's your first move. Use anything sturdy that you can find: logs, corrugated metal, car and truck body panels. Put the shelter in an out-of-the-way place so that it doesn't call attention to itself, but place it nearby something you can flee to—the woods, a park, a junkyard, or an industrial zone. Don't put it in an aqueduct or rail tunnel, or the vampires will simply come at you from either end. Under a bridge or overpass is OK, but bear in mind that the homeless population will be a go-to smorgasbord for the undead, and putting yourself in places where the homeless concentrate opens you to that risk. But if you have homeless comrades, you might form your own compound and defense group. Remember: That homeless guy right next to you might have done some serious shit in Fallujah or God-knows-where-else, and if so, he knows how to handle anything that goes *bang* or *boom*. Share your booze with him.

Build more than one shelter: If you're living outside, you're probably not working full-time, eh? So build yourself another shelter in another good spot, because this will give you a backup location if things get particularly bloody in your usual neighborhood.

Make yourself an indispensable friend to people who have a house: Living the hobo lifestyle is tough enough in regular times. During a vampire uprising, you're finally going to have that bit part in a horror movie you always wanted. So market yourself. What helpful skills might you have to offer to that yuppie couple that can't even figure out how to fix a doorknob in their country home? How might you convince that single mother that she needs a nanny/manny/caretaker/carpenter who's good at killing the undead? Sure, sure—this isn't the moment you thought you'd tie yourself down with another job. But what do you think about free employment (called "slavery") as the valet/wife of a three-hundred-pound ex-death-row-inmate vampire? Get your butt indoors.

Preparing Your Family

Perhaps you have the typical husband-wife-2.5-children domestic situation. Or your family might be you, your aunt, her son, another cousin, a live-in girlfriend, and that guy who works at the gas station who dates your aunt.

Vampires really don't care: **blood is blood.**

What you need from your family during the war against the vampires is commitment, discipline, and the understanding that you've got one another's back. That's family, whether related by blood or not. Oh, yeah, you want some love, too—love helps.

Having the "Talk" with Your Kids

This is going to be easier than the sex talk, because that brings about all kinds of questions about Mommy and Daddy. Vampires give you your best opportunity to explain to your kids "good versus evil" without having to mitigate the notions of "good" or "evil."

With kids under age nine, before you tell them about the coming nights of vampire attacks and what you're going to have to do as a family, maybe read through some of their favorite books—*Where the Wild Things Are, The Care Bears' Big Wish*, or *The Velveteen Rabbit*—to get a sense of who their preferred characters are, and then describe

Vampire Fact:
Numerous vampire myths have to do with the difficulties of childbirth. The Malaysian *lang-suyar* is a beautiful woman who suffered so much pain having a stillborn baby that she turned into a demon that sucked the blood of other women's children. In India, the *churel* or *jakhin* was a woman who died in childbirth (or died an unnatural death). She would return to drink the blood of male family members if her family had mistreated her in life. In Mexico, the Aztec *cihuateteo* is a woman who died in childbirth, and takes a vampire form to attack and paralyze children. The Mexican legend makes specific mention of the fact that sunlight will kill a *cihuateteo*.

vampire attacks in those story terms: "You see, sweetie, when mamma bear saw all those bees trying to take her honey, she had to do something. Vampires are like those bees. They want our honey, and we can't let them have our honey." Just as long as they get the idea that vampires are bad, that they're not going out after dark for a long time, and that the gingersnaps are going to run low for a while, they'll adapt to the rest.

For kids who are a little bit older, say nine to twelve, don't hold back on anything. Kids of this age are starting to get crazy, and if you tell them that they're probably going to see vampires' heads explode, you won't be able to stop them from saying, "Cool!" about a hundred times. After that, they're not going to listen to you, but at least you can say you told them so. Don't show kids of this age how to use weapons—they'll get grabby. But eventually they will learn by watching, and come the third or fourth month of repeated attacks, you can probably trust them to carry your ammo.

Teenagers are a whole other issue. Most likely, vampire uprisings will make them more moody and accentuate their mood swings. In fact, they'll probably be the most difficult people to control (other than the wacko ex-military mercenaries; see chapter 6) unless you have a really good parent-teen relationship. No other book published has ever solved the riddle of teenagers, and this one won't try. But evidence does suggest that teens who have had the total crap scared out of them are a bit more compliant than fearless teens (college-bound or not—doesn't matter). So that really mouthy, rebellious fifteen-year-old you've got? Lock her in a room with a couple vampires you just shot dead. She'll hate you afterward, but she'll do as she's told.

What? You want that "TLC for your teen" approach? Go buy another book—lotta good it will do you when the bloodsuckers are chasing you down the road and your glue-sniffing "honors student" can't run because he cuts gym class—or his school *got rid of gym*.

Spousal Relations

Assuming you are married/shacked up and actually have regular spousal relations before the vampires come a-creepin', how might you keep things cooking in this period of terrible stress?

Stock up on gift cards before the leeches show up: Those "we need to talk" moments are going to be seriously condensed during periods of attack, as there are other pressing matters at hand. Heartfelt notes will help.

Try to have "couples' moments": Between the exhaustion, fear, abject terror, serious physical labor, pervasive violence, hunger and thirst, routine shotgun cleaning, and disposal of vampire bodies, try to schedule ten or fifteen minutes together alone in a side room or on the porch. Maybe you just talk, or rant, or sob uncontrollably, but you'll be sharing as

Random Question: What if my spouse/ significant other fantasizes about a relationship with a vampire?

Vampires have a strong sexual element, both in a literary sense and in person, assuming that the vampire in question looks a lot like Antonio Banderas in *Interview with the Vampire* or Monica Bellucci in *Bram Stoker's Dracula* (yeah, she was in that). Indeed, there will be some really hot vampires. Your spouse's fixation, however, could easily go beyond the imagination: He or she could desire some kind of self-destructive tryst with the undead.

Psychologists and psychotherapists will have all fled to their second homes in gated communities in Martha's Vineyard and the Caribbean, so finding professional help will be out of the question. (Yes, some dedicated psychotherapists will stay in the country, and they'll be swamped with calls and will probably get turned into vampires anyway.) So, you'll have to deal with it yourself.

First, to what degree does your spouse fantasize? Is this a true fantasy, that is, does she know it's ludicrous, but indulges it in a wholly fantastical way? That's merely insulting, not real trouble (for now). Do what you can to shift her undead fantasies to the killer of the undead (you), and you'll find yourself getting some hot lovin'. Maybe dress a little more provocatively, and shoot vampires more than you need to (ammo store providing). Get a little aggressive. Show your passion. Cut off a vampire's head and nail it to the wall, and make sure your spouse sees you do it. She will slowly realize that the desired fantasy figure is a person of action—a dangerous person (not an undead person) and you're it.

But if your spouse really has it in for a vampire, in a psychotic way, you might have to resort to extralegal actions. This will involve duct tape. *Figure it out.*

a couple. Don't try to turn these moments into desperate grapplings for sex. That's for later.

Desperate grapplings for sex: The funny thing about married sex is that one spouse always wants it when the other is tired, doing the laundry, or actively fighting the undead. And the weird thing about vampires is that they can sense the level of a human's sexual frustration or desire and exploit it to their advantage with hypnotic power. Trying to find time for lovemaking during this crisis will be tough, especially if there's no babysitter. You're simply going to have to wait until the kids are asleep, like usual, and until there aren't any vampires sneaking up to the windows. Good luck. Keep your shoes on.

The Family Chain of Command

This is relatively simple: Whoever is paying for everything gets to set the rules and priorities. Don't argue with this, because an epidemic of vampires creates special circumstances. If you think the person in charge (the person who pays the bills) is wrong, make an appeal to the family group and see what everyone decides. Otherwise, the guy or gal who holds the mortgage, lease, or bank account is calling the shots. Democracy is nice, but it's slow, and the vampires ain't going to wait for the next family election. In the daytime, try to build consensus for what's to be done at night, and then the chief has to make the call.

And so what if your father's dumb-ass ideas get everyone killed? He'd already blown your inheritance with risky real-estate investments.

However, the person in charge needs to designate a number two, in the event that a bloodsucker whacks the head of household. When the number two becomes number one, he or she must then choose who's next in line.

Beyond that, the number one needs to give everyone their particular set of duties and must make sure they get carried out. Kids handle cleanup from meals and keep things tidy. Teenagers count ammo and supplies. Adults watch for and fight vampires.

Pets

Vampires are not above drinking the blood of rats, birds, and livestock when times are tough. But with all us corpulent Yanks stuck in our houses, the leeches are going to be thinking that they're never drinking animal blood again (it doesn't have the same bouquet as that of a 260-pound celebrity chef who's stuffed full of truffles, vodka, elk, and cocaine). So by and large, your pets are safe from attack.

What about livestock? The best idea is to put them out in their pastures. Again, the undead will be aiming for people, and aside from a little pointy-fingered cow tipping, the vamps aren't going to pay much attention to outdoor animals. Give your animals room to roam and feed, and do what you can to check on them during the day. The cows and goats will need milking, of course, and if you have them, that's a plus. You can go a long way on water and milk, just ask the bedouin.

Securing Children and Elderly Residents

Those who simply cannot help because they are too young (under age nine) or too old or infirm must be placed in a defendable and securable location. In a house, this is probably an upstairs bedroom with few windows and a strong, lockable door. In an apartment, use a bedroom or possibly the bathroom.

Vampire Fact:
After numerous cases of vampirism in Serbia in the early 1700s, the word *vampyre* entered the English lexicon in 1734, via translations of official investigations. The first literary vampire story in English was *The Vampyre,* by John Polidori, published in 1819 and attributed initially to Lord Byron.

Creating an Anti-Vampire Network

Dire situations have an effect on friendships and associations. On the one hand, they can fuse and solidify honorable, lifelong bonds. On the other hand, they also can cause an individual to manipulate and coerce everyone in his path. What you do and say during the fight against the vampires will be your legacy if you survive.

Who Do You Know?

The first people you want to talk to are your neighbors. Neighbors fall into three categories: Those you like, those you don't like, and those you don't know. You need to be pragmatic about all of them. Those fun neighbors who let you use their swimming pool might turn into needy freaks when the blood starts squirting. The unfriendly couple with the ugly dogs? Turns out they own an ammunition company. The people you don't know? Make contact, check them out, maybe leave your number and get theirs—you might both need to help each other down the line. At the very least, you make yourself known and if you're at all organized and determined, you might at least give the impression that you're not to be trifled with.

As for the police or any security agents, if you know a few, ask them for their advice about securing your home or apartment. There's no need to let on much more about your situation than that. Given that curfews and, in some places, martial law will take effect, having a few police friends is a good idea, but no one's really going to worry about protecting your individual rights but you.

After that, flip through your Rolodex. Any high-powered agents? Celebrities? Politicians? Media professionals? Get in touch: Leave a voice mail or send an e-mail. With the way the whacky media world works these days, you never know when CNN or MTV might want to do a segment on a family battling vampires by night and growing organic foods by day (your big plans to reduce your carbon emissions are going to take a hit when you start torching dead vampires). The exposure might help, either in the form of attention to your situation, if desperate, or help after the uprising is quelled and you're looking for a new job because they fired your ass from the organic grocery store when you refused to dispose of vampires the "organic way" using cheese molds.

Who Owes You a Favor?

This is going to have to be a substantial favor, not some I-gave-you-a-ride-to-the-airport crap. You kept someone out of jail. You covered for a cheating spouse. You handed someone any amount over five hundred dollars and told her to pay it back whenever she could. You let someone sleep on your sofa rent-free for over two months. Who knows what you'll need this person for—extra team member, help setting traps—but when the chips are down, don't be shy about calling it in. But you'll have to wipe the slate clean when the favor is returned. So if you loaned that slacker cousin of your husband six hundred dollars to cover a gambling debt, then you better pull seven hundred dollars' worth of labor out of that guy.

Who Can You Help?

This isn't about the "let me know if I can help" kind of thing you say over the phone to people you're kissing up to. This is about providing something actual and substantial: calling the cops or the National Guard to report the movements of looters, prowlers, or vampires. Helping a good neighbor fortify his home as well as yours, knowing you can hide there safely and vice versa. Sticking your neck out to provide suppressing fire with anti-vampire forces as they move through your neighborhood. Serving with a worthwhile, effective volunteer home guard during the daylight hours, knowing you can call on them if things get bad. Slipping friends a little extra ammo, food, liquor, or information here and there can't hurt.

Vampire Fact:
Coffins are not a necessity of vampirism. Vampires can rest almost anywhere, much like humans. The bloodsuckers of early Western vampire literature—Varney, Carmilla, Lord Ruthven—did not rest in coffins. Dracula (in the novel) had to rest in his native soil, but not necessarily in a coffin. The idea that the coffin is the essential resting place derives from the 1931 Hollywood film version of *Dracula*.

Creating Lines of Communication

Find out who's staying in nearby houses or apartments in your building. Get their numbers and e-mail addresses, and create "phone trees" just like they did back in the dark ages before text messages, when one person called four people on the list to let them know the office was closed due to snow or a national emergency like the big ghoul panic of 1988 (it was somehow connected to the savings and loan scandal). When one person sees vampires, or just fights off a few without killing them, he calls the people on his list and tells them what's going on, and then they call their designated contacts. Track these calls in a written and digital log.

In the daytime, have regular meetings to compare notes. Who's seen what? Who shot what? Who's heard what? Chart this as well.

Assembling Your Vampire Fighters

America has become a socially fractured place. Families are separated by demanding jobs, military deployments, divorce, and endless distractions. Just like cable television, people are categorized into specific groups, united by niche interests. Perhaps the only things that unite Americans in big groups anymore are politics, religion, and sports.

So the idea of a "party" or a "team" is crucial during vampire uprisings, as defending your home alone or just as a couple is difficult, especially so for small, young families (parents and a few kids under twelve). In regions where uprisings are rampant and last for weeks or more, creating defendable homes by bringing together two or three families, groups of relatives, or a bunch of friends and coworkers is going to be necessary.

Average people learn about close-quarters combat from TV and movies. Few people have read the *Ranger Unit Operations Field Manual*, or *The SAS Combat Handbook*. If you want to consult military manuals, that's fine—they'll give you some useful ideas and tactics. But they're written for highly trained specialists in great physical condition, not us regular folks.

What is offered here is, at best, a basic approach, intended first and foremost to prevent people from shooting one another, because that will be, at times, a larger danger than the vampires themselves (assuming your house is well fortified). The following scenarios assume a few basics: one, that there are at least three armed adults or older adolescents in the home; two, everyone has agreed to a chain of command and decision making; three, everyone is committed to defending the home and everyone in it.

Vampires can see well enough in the dark that there's no sense keeping all the lights turned off. Most researchers agree that many vampires have some infrared capabilities and pick up your heat signature. So if you don't have night-vision optics, illuminate your house sufficiently at night.

Watch Team

The watch team is everyone—every member of the household or hideout is given a window or door to watch. If there aren't enough people to cover all the spots, you'll have to pick essential posts—those with the widest field of view—and stick with them, circulating occasionally to other posts. Every member of the watch team should be armed, but avoid shooting anything until a leech is actually making its way in (unless you have set up the shooting perches discussed below).

When a person spots a vampire outside, she or he should quietly alert everyone else by a flashlight signal, a low whistle, or some other relatively quiet signal. At this point, follow a previously outlined course of action, the best one being to do nothing and let the bloodsuckers continue to roam.

Again, depending upon how many people you have, the watch team can work in shifts so that everyone gets sufficient rest. The human body is naturally programmed to want to sleep in the dark. Sometimes, exhaustion cannot be beat, and getting sleep is essential. If you don't have enough people to cover everything during irresistible periods of sleepiness, place sleepers in secure locations, and have at least one person who's awake stationed at the best vantage point for watching outside.

What the vampires are doing: In early evening, the blood-suckers get moving, looking for easy pickings—mini-mizing effort for maximum return, just like any predator. They'll take the first hours of darkness to reconnoi-ter their territory, looking for changes in human habits or houses (fortifications that have fallen off or houses where people are active). They will keep themselves con-cealed during these quick patrols, but soon enough they

will venture closer to homes to look for ways in and get a sense of who is home. By midnight, the bloodsuckers will need to feed.

Spotter and Shooter Team

The home-invading vampire knows that it must make a quick and quiet entry. Total quiet is not always possible, and a vampire will opt for speed if it thinks it can get into a dark room and then quickly move to another part of the house; if this means breaking a window frame, or cracking through the bottom or edge of a door, a vampire that's hungry enough will do so.

You'll need to set up a spotter and shooter team to provide a ballistic reception for vampires determined to crash through a door or window. This three-person team consists of two shooters and the person operating a spotlight or a very strong flashlight. One person is shooter number one, the main shooter; the other is the backup. The spotter always stands behind both shooters. Shooter number one can be in a forward position, with his backup directly behind him or in line with him in a secondary position (against the wall or behind furniture).

As the vampire breaks through a door, window, or weakened wall, the spotter lights it up with the spotlight or flashlight. Vampires' eyes are sensitive to very bright direct light and this can momentarily baffle them. Spotlight the vamp in the face as soon as its head is visible and keep the light on it.

Shooter number one should call, "Fire!" before he or she shoots to let everyone know lead is going to fly—but number two does not shoot yet. The backup waits until number one is out of ammo or has a problem. In that case, the number one calls out, "Backup shooter," and the backup opens fire. The spotter keeps the light on the vampire at all times.

This setup works for single vampires, or up to three vampires. You can practice it in a barn or garage, but live-fire practice is not recommended unless you can set up an outdoor practice range.

Yes, you're thinking: What if four or five vampires come crashing through a window at once? In that case, the number one shooter calls out, "Free fire!" and both he and number two unload. In this scenario, the person with nerves of steel is the spotlighter, who must keep the non-buckshot-firing spotlight in place and not waver.

You will be surprised how many people do not fortify their homes sufficiently when reports of vampires in their area start to surface. If you're one of them, pay close attention to scuffling, sliding, or scratching sounds—the kinds of noises you might attribute to mice, pigeons, or stray cats. Pay especially close attention to your dog, and take heed if he's bugging out.

Recon and Repair Team

Depending upon how many people are in your house, once the shooting is over, a second two- or three-person team, recon and repair, should scout the outer perimeter from the windows and/or doors, and call out "All clear!" when appropriate. While the shooter team stays on alert at the point of entry, two people from recon and repair should close and refortify the door or window that was bashed open. Everyone should return to their watch position after repairs are made.

Vampires outside the house, near and at a distance, will have heard the shooting and will be attracted by it, out of curiosity and hunting instinct; the humans who fired the shots might not be ready for another attack so soon. Expect to be quickly scoped out by the leeches after you plug one of their own.

If you've noticed a lot of vampire activity and have already shot a few, it is safe to assume that others are still lurking nearby. These vampires might simply move off, given the reception their compadres received. Or they might linger, watch, and plan a subsequent attack on a different part of the house.

Anti-Vampire Reconnaissance

In addition to a log of family or team activity, vampire visits and attacks, and vampire killings, you might also maintain a "data map" of your town or county. You'll have to rely on your network for this, and at least a weekly meeting to compile your friends' and neighbors' information will be necessary.

The object is to create a map that charts vampire movement, sightings, and killings to help you discern the patterns, movements, and activities of the undead. At first, it might seem to be a totally random and unremarkable pattern—"They're everywhere!" your friends will say—and, indeed, the vampires might have gone everywhere. But by careful study, you should be able to determine which direction they from come at sundown, which direction they retreat to near dawn, the parts of the neighborhood or town to which they gravitate, and the areas they appear to be attacking the most at any given moment. Figuring out the "whys" of these questions can help you to build more coordinated anti-vampire defenses and blast a few more every week.

Selecting and Creating a Hunter Team

If your home-defense efforts go well, you might consider creating a hunter team. This calls for a bit more depth than a shooting team that operates within the confines of a secure home or on brief outdoor efforts combined with traps. This is about roving around your 'hood looking for trouble. Attempt this only in sparsely populated places and neighborhoods that have been mostly evacuated. Ostensibly, this is an offensive night-time action, but you can also go a-roving with your hunting team during the day, looking to flush out resting vampires, although this will involve getting quite close to them and will be akin to hunting rattlesnakes. Big rattlesnakes.

If you have friends in your circle who have police training, are military veterans, or have successfully done some seriously dangerous hunting, these are the people to collect for such an endeavor, provided they are willing. If they're willing but also litigious types, you might consider having them sign a release form or at least some kind of pledge. Hey, you don't want to welcome in a vampire-free summer by getting subpoenaed in a *wrongful-death suit,* do you?

Put together two teams of three or four people, each with at least one highly experienced member. When you can, in the daytime, perform some practice drills:

Forming and moving as a phalanx: The "phalanx" is a 360-degree protective cover formation, with a three-person team in a twelve o'clock/four o'clock/eight o'clock configuration, and a four-person team in a twelve o'clock/three o'clock/six o'clock/nine o'clock configuration. Practice moving over uneven ground in this setup, carrying all essential equipment, including firearms (do not practice with loaded firearms). The phalanx need not be perfect as the team moves, though at least one person should have eyes on the rearward view. But when the team takes and holds a position for a while, each member should be alert and looking in the correct direction. The team leader is always forward, in the twelve o'clock of the phalanx, and directions are based on his right or left.

Calling, spotting, and shooting targets: When a team member sees a vampire, he quietly reports its position: "Leech on our three o'clock." Whoever is at that position gets ready to shoot, while the six o'clock person readies a spotlight. The six o'clock man is the spotlighter for both three o'clock and nine o'clock. The three o'clock man is the spotlighter for six o'clock and twelve o'clock. When a team member gets ready to shoot, the two unengaged members stay at their positions, facing out and watching. Only if the shooter or the spotlighter calls out for backup should the other team members turn. This is in case the team has stumbled into a setup of two or more bloodsuckers and faces multiple targets. As ever: Shoot for center mass.

Night Patrol: Taking the Fight to the Undead

As a team leader, plot out your patrol and stick to it. Do this on a street-level map, preferably a topographic one so you know when you'll be shooting up- or downhill (you might have to superimpose a street map on a topo-map). Take the map with you but make an effort to memorize it and be able to see your route clearly in your head. Review the route with everyone in the teams (a night patrol should always contain at least two teams; you can't do it with just one).

Don't patrol all night. Pick a route, cover it in a specific amount of time, and return home. Obviously, this kind of operation cannot be seriously undertaken without a home occupied by at least a dozen people, as a skeleton crew will have to remain in the home. If you completely vacate a house, you compromise whatever security you've created there, and a vampire could penetrate it and be waiting in your empty house for your return.

Also, be sure to inform select friends and contacts about the patrol, including your local cop contact (who will most likely advise against it). You risk the possibility of this information getting to the vampires, but you want to prevent accidental shootings.

As for the actual patrol:

Leap-frog your way. Move a short distance very slowly, and then sit and listen for a brief time, perhaps twenty minutes, and then move a short distance again, slowly. You can speed that up a bit, but that's how you should leapfrog your way: Cover ground, then arrive at an observation/listening post and sit there for some time. These positions should be worked out on the map beforehand so that the two teams will sit near each other, but not in each other's line of fire. Time everything and mark it on the map: Two minutes to move from position A to B, three minutes to move from B to C. Sit for ten minutes at position A, twenty minutes at position B. And so forth. Both teams should move at the same time. Saying you should be on full alert is obvious, but be especially careful when you take up a new position, as you might just come upon a hiding vampire.

Maintain radio or cell-phone contact. Have radio checks at predetermined points, but by all means use your communication systems whenever necessary to alert the other team to anything important (strange noises, structures or objects, tracks).

Stick to public places. Cutting through backyards is asking for trouble, unless you've called ahead. Patrol only on streets and public property.

Wear appropriate clothing. Just like the vampires them-selves, you'll want to favor quiet, dark, and dull-shaded clothing, like dark gray, olive-drab, or blue. True black stands out too much, especially in periods of moonlight, so avoid it. Dress warmly as necessary but with the ability to vent body heat if you go out in early or mid-spring. Wear good, comfortable, durable boots or trail shoes. Wear a hat, or, if you feel like it, a helmet.

Essential equipment to carry:

1. At least once team member should have a device that can be used to signal the other team silently and indi-cate your position and the fact that you're a friendly. A halogen flashlight with a blue- or red-bulb setting works fine. Don't use a laser, as that suggests some kind of targeting device and will cause havoc.
2. Two first-aid kits per team.
3. A flare gun. In the event that a team realizes they are un-der attack from multiple vampires, they should send up a flare, which will do two things: Illuminate the blood-suckers and give everyone better visuals, and alert the other team to your location and dire predicament.

Patrol: Bad Stuff 1

If a vampire spots your patrol before you spot it, it will more than likely avoid you. It wants blood more than it wants a fight. But an aggressive or highly capable vampire (like, say, an ol' Spetsnaz guy who got transformed during the war in Chechnya) will begin to stalk the team. It will try to get ahead of you and then let you come to it, and, from a concealed position, it will snatch a team member and make off quickly, rushing into an alleyway or thick brush, and everyone will (should) be too afraid of accidentally shooting the abducted team member to actually crank off a round. You will have no choice but to give pursuit. Call in the other team, and stay hot after the bloodsucker, but stay together—don't get strung out. One of four bad things will come of this: You will find your team member drained of most of his blood but alive. You will find your team member dead or dying. You won't find your team member. You will find part of your team member. But you're not going to get a shot at that vampire. He burned your asses.

Vampire Fact:

There have been numerous cases of "criminal vampirism" in which a person is gripped by *hematomania*: the need for sexual and other pleasures to be satisfied by drinking or bathing in human blood. Some hematomaniacs obtain human blood from willing donors, while others kill for it. The famous German hematomaniac Fritz Haarmann murdered, cannibalized, and also drank the blood of some of his twenty victims before his execution in 1924. In 1967, American seaman James Brown killed and drank the blood of two fellow sailors on board their ship. Imprisoned in Massachusetts, he killed two more people and drank their blood, earning himself a padded cell in the National Asylum in Washington, D.C. Brazilian Marcelo de Andrade was nabbed in 1991 for the murders of fourteen boys; he reportedly drank their blood and ate their flesh.

SCOTT BOWEN

Patrol: Bad Stuff 2

You shoot a bloodsucker but not very well and it runs off. Soon after that you shoot another, killing this one. And someone in your team says, "Not the same guy, but he's wearing the exact same jacket." *Oh snap!* That's the sign that you're engaging members of a coven, or at least a loosely formed gang of new or younger vampires. And if you've met two, you're about to meet the rest. Seriously haul ass, right now. If the coven swarms you, however, stay in the phalanx formation, get your guns up, spotlights on, and start shooting. They will come at you like blitzing linebackers, and you'll have to keep your cool. The main thing is to take up a defendable position: Don't get into a shootout in the middle of the street, parking lot, or field; get cover on at least one side.

This is a quick-and-dirty description of forming and operating a hunter team. Remember, you do this by your own choice and at extreme risk.

The Vampire Black Market

Sometimes you can't get everything you need at Wal-Mart, like, say, dynamite and blasting caps. Rest assured that during this period of bloodsucking chaos, a very active and reasonably accessible black market is going to spring up in various places. Here, cash and barter are the only forms of exchange, and prices can be steep. The black market will trade in both specialized and highly popular items: liquor, drugs (prescription and illicit), gourmet foods, knockoff designer fashions, weapons and ammunition, illegal forms of identification, various vehicles (want a Ducati with a built-in Mac-10?), and livestock. Dealing with black-market people won't be a picnic—they're not always the most upstanding citizens—but they are also often very well connected and can offer another precious commodity: information.

The black market can also afford you a chance to make some serious cash, because there will be several vampire-specific trades into which you can venture (just don't let the leeches know):

Celebrity vampire bodies: If you have the odd luck of killing a celebrity vampire (see chapter 6), there are people who will pay serious money for that dead red-carpet bloodsucker. Why? Because there are some seriously creepy people who will embalm celebrity vampires, even B-list celebs and popular media-attention whores, and set them up in life-size vampire dioramas in their homes. An A-list vampire, on roughly a rap-star or regular film-star level, might get you $10,000. A total B-lister vampire might fetch $3,000.

Vampire skulls, hands, teeth, and other body parts: Entire new occult interests in vampire artifacts will develop during the uprising. Plenty of voodoo-juju types are going to try to use vampire parts as instruments of divination or to assimilate vampire power unto themselves. A good, intact vampire skull might fetch $500. Just move it quickly.

Vampire clothes, tools, and jewelry: Serious collectors of vampire artifacts who are reticent to possess actual body parts will be happy to purchase what you, the vampire killer,

---

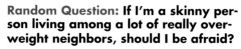

Random Question: If I'm a skinny person living among a lot of really overweight neighbors, should I be afraid?

Before you get feeling all superior about your thin-person genes, or your yoga routine, or your incredibly disciplined anorexia, ask yourself if you happen to know how to handle a Remington 870 pump-action better than the fat guy next door. Because if you don't, you better damn well bake that guy a nice big cake and ask if you might hang out in his rec room for the next six months.

Being skinny won't necessarily save you in any given situation, and if you live in a vampire-attracting demographic, then you're going to face the same onslaught that's making your chubby friends and neighbors sweat through their XXL team shirts.

Vampires that find a size 2 amid a bunch of size 16s won't mistake you for Kate Moss, and unless they sense that your blood might taste bad due to disease (jaundice, hepatitis, leukemia, anemia, and kidney disease can all alter the flavor of blood), you're fair game, whether you still fit into your prom dress or not.

take off the body of a blasted leech. Vampire-made materials and implements are visibly different from contemporary human design and manufacture. Some vampires might
opt to use human-made clothes or tools for a time but will
customize them in their own way. Human vampire killers,
social clubs, researchers, rock bands, artists, and vampires
themselves will pay for these things. Again, if you do collect this stuff, unload it rapidly and quietly, and only after
you've made effective black-market contacts. But in this
respect you can't deny the *blam-ka-ching-blam* sound your
gun makes.

Human blood: A single unit (450 ml) of whole human
blood sold for roughly $300, for laboratory work, before
the uprisings began. At the height of the uprisings, nation-
wide, a unit of whole blood might go for $400, because of
increased demand. A truly capitalist human-vampire interaction will create a thriving blood-sale sector of the black
market, in which those humans who collect blood will sell
it to vampire intermediaries and sometimes directly to vampires, which will carry the blood while they travel, allowing them to continue to enjoy human blood while they lie
low to observe a new group of victims before attacking. The
usual anti-coagulants used in blood storage are foul-tasting
to the vampire palate, so blood sold to the leeches can't be
more than two hours old, another factor that will drive up
the price. Here's the real question: Could you sell a unit
of your own blood for $50 to a black marketeer, and then
knowingly shoot the vampire who drank it?

Vampire Fact:

France lacks any significant vampire folklore, but one French nobleman, Viscount de Morière, has been cited as an actual vampire. Morière managed to hang on to his estate during the French Revolution, but after the political upheaval, he began to execute his employees as revenge against the class of people who would have otherwise guillotined him. This led to his assassination. Not long after his death, several young children died suddenly, each of them appearing to have been bitten. For the next seventy years, rumors swirled that the (undead) viscount was somehow involved in the many unexpected child deaths that continued in the area. Eventually, Morière's grandson decided to find out the truth. He opened the family tomb with town officials in tow, and they saw that every other body had decayed, but the viscount's appeared entirely intact, the fingernails grown, the skin fresh. Morière's grandson had a white thorn driven into his grandfather's heart, and his body cremated. The child deaths came to an end.

Chapter 5
The Gathering Doom

The bloodsuckers are not going to arrive loudly like an army or stampede of wild horses. Imagine them more like a smog or chemical weapon, slowly spreading and largely invisible. While there will be times when they attempt to actually smash their way into homes or other structures, they will be immensely stealthy overall—a combination of panther, snake, bat, and ninja. In general, they will want to preserve the availability and quality of the blood feast for as long as they can. For some, especially groups and covens, that will mean abducting humans and holding them like livestock. Other vampires will feed furtively, pouncing on and overwhelming victims, or hypnotizing and seducing them, and biting, sucking, and leaving.

Uprisings will not occur in a coordinated fashion. Across localities and regions, vampire activity will simply start to rise quickly and sharply, as individual leeches or small groups of vampires sense their increasing activity overall, the way animals become aware of the movements of their own kind.

Vampires will also move across significant areas, traveling across entire states or regions. Weeks or even months of vampire attacks may be followed by a complete lull, and then more vampires could arrive and the cycle will start again. This will not be tied to seasons, moon phases, or anything else except the vampires' manifest desire for a period of gluttony. So if you live in an area that has experienced increased vampire activity, expect this to happen again.

Whenever they can, vampires will travel along remote corridors—forest or agricultural areas and empty coastlines—as Nightstalkers special-ops chopper crews (160th Special Operations Group) and secret FBI countervampire teams will be doing their best to track the leeches. Some measures will be taken to stop roving vampires before they reach major population centers, but the vampires' ability to avoid detection and interdiction is renowned. Many will get through whatever screen the bureaucracies that run our security forces can manage to put up.

You are the last line of defense.

The Vampires' First Move

Many of the undead will be traveling on foot. But a significant number of vampires will have cars and aircraft, using these to proceed to the buffet of their choice. A big rumor in a lot of vampiric chat rooms is that some major hipster-trash vampires are going to fly from New York to Miami, then Las Vegas, and finally L.A., sucking down the *sangre* all the way, making the old MGM Grand New York to L.A. party flight look like a Baptist mission. Russian vampire gangsters from Brooklyn are supposed to try to make fast moves to take over Atlantic City, but not if the south Philly blood-and-cheese-steak gang has anything to say about it.

But the majority of the vampire horde will not be distracted by socializing or organized criminality—they will seek out good sources of blood with direct, deeply intense concentration.

High-Yield Blood-Feast Demographics

As this period of uprising is about food, vampires are going to travel toward and amass around the best sources of abundant blood. This means the bigger cities and most populated regions, the fattest cities, and the fattest states. The top-twenty fattest cities in America include Chicago, Las Vegas, Los Angeles, Dallas, Houston, Memphis, Long Beach, El Paso, Kansas City, Detroit, Cleveland, Philadelphia, and Indianapolis. The entire Midwest from North Dakota to Texas, and the entire South from Arkansas to Florida make up the fattest region; the three fattest states are Mississippi, Alabama, and West Virginia (according to average body mass index). In the West, the fattest states are Oregon and Nevada. Boston, Miami, New York City, and Washington, D.C., will also see large numbers of vampires.

Residents of these cities and states need to map out their areas and locate nearby state parks, national forests, river corridors, ports, and industrial areas. Mark those and avoid them, as the undead will be using them as observation posts, assembly points, and places to rest during the day.

Roughly half of the vampires will aim for urban centers first, and then move steadily outward into the suburbs and rural regions. The rest will avoid the heavily populated and defended cities and plan their attack for smaller towns and outlying counties that are worth the chase.

A word about Colorado: This is the state that has the lowest body mass index of the entire country. This can't be due entirely to a lesser population, as lately everyone is moving to the Boulder State: Colorado's population has grown by 25 percent in the past decade. What might be truer is that the people already there are used to a rugged lifestyle, and those who move there are seeking a rugged lifestyle. It's an athletic state, with lots of snow sports, rock-climbing, trekking, hunting, fishing, and the Olympic Training Center in Colorado Springs. Plus, there's a lot of open space, and, to be candid, a lot of firearms and commensurate numbers of people who are very good with them. Colorado is not the place for vampires, though a number that like a challenge will show up.

Vampire Fact:
Possibly the most gruesome vampire-like entity of folklore is the Malaysian *penanggalan*, composed of a woman's bodiless head from which dangle the still-attached esophagus, stomach, and entrails. This gory head floats and flies at will. If the dripping blood from the *penanggalan*'s dangling guts falls on you, it causes illness. This evil thing appears at houses where women are giving birth or where babies sleep, intending to suck their blood.

Mass Vampire Movements in the Dark

After the first outbreak of vampire attacks, many of the bloodsuckers will go on the move. Long-separated members of covens will seek to reunite, and new associations will form in the truly frightening days leading up to the maximum bloodletting. While police and various security forces will be on the lookout for vampire movements, you can make some easy observations during the day:

- Look for areas that have clearly been walked through by groups, in places were few people go in numbers, such as riverbanks, remote agricultural areas, and abandoned factory or institutional grounds.
- Check abandoned houses, warehouses, and structures to see if they have been entered—doors, shutters, or siding might have been pulled off. Take note of any bloodstains in or around these structures.
- Watch for dead or visibly weakened livestock. Vampires are known to feed on cows and horses as they travel.
- Listen for reports of missing homeless people. They will quickly fall victim.
- Check for signs of intruders around your home and property if you live in rural or out-of-the-way places.
- Rescue slow-moving elderly people with visible bites.

Getting Up Close

In the days before they begin full-on hunting, the vampires will station themselves close to city centers and populated areas. They will take up residence in abandoned houses, empty warehouses, empty railcars, and underground storage spaces. The undead will press right up to the edges of neighborhoods. As reports of attacks and deaths in the nearest major town become last week's news, your situation will become critical—by now you should have a secured shelter and all the supplies and weapons you need.

The vampires have arrived.

Rural, Suburban, and Urban Survival Situations

Cities will provide the best nutrients-to-vampire ratio, but vampires will also happily go to work in Moon-Pie Town or BMWville, and take their time. Smug suburbanites who now consider themselves "healthily overweight" will find lots of their own pork-rich blood staining their designer rugs. Tougher American brethren out in the countryside will be hand-loading their own special-recipe buckshot shells.

Vampires in the Countryside

Rural areas afford vampires a lot of advantages: limited police, lots of places to hide and rest, a populace cut off from bureaucratic centers, and the chance of going undetected for significant periods of time. The disadvantages are a populace used to fending for themselves, reactionary behavior toward outsiders, and lots of dogs.

Citizens of the rural places would do well to do the following:

- Create several strong, centrally located shelters in churches, businesses, and farms with multiple structures, and occupy these with as many people as possible. Create a chain of command and determine a strategy for defending these places.
- Travel during the daytime and only in open places. This is a universal rule during periods of roving vampires, but taking a shortcut down Dismal Dark Swamp Road on a cloudy day is just asking for it, even in daylight hours.
- Identify places were vampires might congregate—abandoned farms, dense woods, caves—and mark these as off-limits. If you assemble a vampire-hunter team (see chapter 4), you might flush these out on sunny days.
- Corral livestock, thus depriving the undead of a ready food source, if you're able to attend to your livestock regularly. You can also use livestock as bait in vampire traps: Set up guards on corrals at night and expect travel-weary and hungry vampires to make an attempt. Put a shooter team in a hayloft overlooking the livestock, and have a number one shooter with a carbine or rifle, and a spotlighter at the ready.

Cul-de-sac Bloodbath

If there's one trait about the suburbs, it's that the residents there, as a group, can't agree on anything. Everyone thinks he's smarter than that jerk across the street or the cabbage-head who's the chairman of the zoning board. What arises in the suburbs, again and again, is a bureaucratic version of high school social politics, but with master plans, property taxes, and sewers thrown in.

Oh, and vampires—they should be there anytime soon, too.

Given that agreement on procedure will be at a minimum in most suburbs, do yourself a favor and take these measures:

- Organize your friends and reasonable neighbors into a local home guard. Set up contact with friends in other neighborhoods and establish direct travel routes to them. Be ready to take shelter with them, and vice versa.
- Get to know the mayor, chief of police, and director of public safety and quickly assess their limitations. You will most likely have to dismiss these people entirely.
- Make contact with cops who might stay on patrol. Let them know how they can rely on you.
- Do not advertise how many supplies or how much water you have stockpiled—you don't want human gate crashers right now.

A-Train to Exsanguination

Whether your city is one of the top twenty fattest in the nation or not, it will attract vampires by the thousands. People in cities tend to go out at night, they tend to party, they tend to hang out with people they don't really know, and they tend to end up in apartments they've never been to before, watching some guy with Maori tattoos suck blood out of their arm.

If you're a city dweller, an uprising is going to be a tough time (as if it ain't elsewhere). Employers are going to insist you get into the office. ("There are no vampires on the freeway/subway/beltway—get your ass in here *now*!") There will be the requisite amount of panic. And cops and "other government organizations" are going to be frisking at random without asking questions. Think of it as a really downer New Year's Eve mixed with a badly done citywide security drill (if you were in NYC for the '04 Republican National Convention, you've got a pretty good idea already).

But urbanites, take heart—there are many things you can do to help yourself:

- Avoid the waterfront and industrial areas. Vampires will congregate in those places.
- If your city has a rapid-transit system—MARTA, the Loop, or a subway—avoid it at night. Really—talk about a movable feast.

- Avoid the upper floors of the tallest buildings. Vampires will be using these as observation posts. They will be using rifle scopes and binoculars to watch the streets below. Security forces will also target these upper floors, and there's no sense dying in the crossfire just because you want to show your date the lights of the Walt Whitman Bridge.

- Keep in touch with other people in your building and on your street, and be on alert for the nights when the bloodsuckers are haunting your 'hood.

- Urban curfews will kill most nightlife, but if you find work in an underground after-hours club or restaurant, you're going to find out exactly what kind of survival skills you have. Get to know taxi drivers who usually drive your streets. Get to know the beat cops (yeah, you had some hassles with them a while ago, but now you need to talk to them). Make contact with other people who get off work at the same time or who frequent the same clubs, and make plans to get home as a group. Hey, you might meet someone nice.

- Arming yourself in the city is a dicey proposition. Cops are going to enforce gun laws, for the most part,

Vampire Fact:

After the divergence of the Christian churches in 1054, the Latin (Catholic) and Greek (Eastern Orthodox) churches took radically different views of the corruption or incorruption of dead bodies. In the Catholic view, the incorruption of a dead body was an indication of saintliness. In the Eastern Orthodox view, any such lack of bodily decay was a sign of the undead.

Random Question: Are these vampire uprisings actually just another government plot, like the assassination of Kennedy, the fake moon landings, the Ronald Reagan robot, and 9/11?

Ah, the old Ronald Reagan robot—how quaint he seems now. Imagine what they could have done with today's animatronics.

Unfortunately, the vampires are real. They might not seem real yet, but they will. See, unlike all those other things that you mentioned, which may or may not have been "government plots," multiple vampire uprisings are not a single incident at a specific time that can be scripted and coordinated (assuming that each moon landing can be considered a specific, discrete event). These country-wide incidents are simply too extensive to be a devilish government operation. They will involve too many different people, alive and undead, across too wide an area to be a "plan" or "program." But will there be government malfeasance, lack of oversight, corruption, cover-ups, secrecy, spying, error, and misinformation? Why, yes, of course.

How will you know it's real? When people you trust start telling you things that seem totally outrageous, like, "Dave Matthews's music is so great, and I'd swear some woman bit me on the neck last night while I walked home and I didn't even know her," or, "I saw a large, strange, pale man in a field drinking blood out of a horse's severed head, but I didn't stop because I was in a hurry to go see the new Robin Williams movie."

How will you know it's *really* real? From the acute pain of fangs piercing your skin.

unless all hell breaks loose (quite possible) and they're battling the undead left and right, and the urban populace will be on its own for a while (you might want to watch *Fort Apache*, *The Warriors,* and *Escape from New York* again, just for pointers). But carrying a concealed gun is most likely a bad idea—your chances of getting searched are much higher than your chances of shooting your way out of a vampire encounter. But in your apartment or townhouse, have anything you want. Have you heard about the Benelli M1?

What the Government Will and Won't Do

Plenty of people think the moon landings were fake; they'll think the vampire uprisings are also fake—right up to the point that they're hanging upside down while a bunch of teenage vampires guzzle the blood streaming from the holes in their neck. But you're not wrong to take what federal and state government *tell* you about an uprising with a big grain of salt. The actual governmental reaction to these uprisings, however, should differ little, regardless of which party holds power.

The Politicos

Republicans will vocally worry about how vampire uprisings might raise taxes. They will decry the notion of a "vampire tax," despite the fact that millions will be needed to fight what's coming. They will blame other countries for what is happening, will call for a national day of prayer, and will brand the vampires as "the ultimate illegal aliens." Democrats will exhort everyone to be careful of resorting to violence, to reach out to families and neighbors they don't know, and to realize that the only successful way to combat vampirism is through an understanding of the disease itself. The Libertarians will decry any federal effort to combat the uprisings and push for billions in taxes to be repaid so that individual Americans will be able to afford to fight the undead properly. The American Green Party will ask Americans not to burn vampire bodies, thus creating huge releases of carbon, but to put dead undead through wood chippers. The Workers' Party will lobby Congress to pass legislation allowing for twelve weeks "paid crisis leave" for every American employee. The LaRouchies will declare war on Slovenia and China, saying these countries are the sources of vampirism in the Western and Eastern worlds, respectively, and assert that the queen of England is a dangerous vampire.

In concert, the executive and legislative branches will:

- Move the state of alert to DEFCON 3.
- Recall as many Special Forces groups from abroad as possible.
- Revive the Alien and Sedition Acts, and suspend *habeas corpus*.
- Create emergency funding (it will pass Congress in a

voice vote).
- Ignore the $9.2 trillion national debt.
- Raise all taxes immediately.
- Make June 7 "The Living Americans' National Freedom Day," otherwise known as "Shoot-a-Vampire Day."
- Provide federal funds for privately run prisons for vampires.

Random Question: To what extent can people rely on fire departments and EMTs during a vampire uprising?

Nighttime fires and emergencies will be dicey during a period of vampire uprising. In small towns with largely volunteer forces, a timely response from the FD or the ambulance squad will be highly doubtful. Fire departments in larger areas, with decent police and military presence, will probably be able to respond at night to house fires, given the fact that fire brings lots of humans and repels vampires. But EMT squads in many places will have their hands full with bite victims and folks suffering vampiric transformation (fire departments that are first responders will have the same problem). Those terrific dilemmas will compete with the usual heart attacks, strokes, and gunshot wounds. Bottom line: American human mortality in general will rise significantly, either due to vampire attack or death from natural causes or injuries that could not be attended to during the uprising.

State Government

You might be able to rely on state government a bit more than the feds, assuming that your state is not over twenty million dollars in debt, has an approved budget, has a governor with good connections to the White House, and has a state police force that approved their contract. Otherwise, expect:

- Early calm and clarity from the statehouse that wanes quickly after the first week of the crisis.
- Vampires posing as land developers trying to lobby legislators during nighttime sessions.
- Grim warnings about your state pension fund.
- Very short lines at the DMV.

The FBI, the CIA, the NSA, and the CDC

As big an embarrassment as September 11, 2001, was for our security forces, the dereliction was at the top. Rank-and-file agents at a number of agencies were yelling and screaming about the very real terrorist threat for months, with little real effect. Now, again, the effectiveness of the security reaction to the vampire uprisings will be mitigated by politics and bureaucratic systems.

The FBI

The job of the FBI is to fight foreign intelligence operations in the United States, wage counterterrorism programs, combat organized and major violent crime, and fight cyber crime, among many other duties. Justice Department lawyers have labeled vampire uprisings as crime waves, of sorts—waves of assault, rape, murder, kidnapping, and

violations of various federal laws that classify the knowing transfer of a dangerous disease as a felony—all caused
by toxic entities that posses no further legal rights than the
disease itself. This makes the killing of vampires a wholly
legal act, akin to killing poultry infected with avian flu. The
JD also ruled that the undead are akin to deceased persons,
and therefore cannot be "killed" in the legal understanding of killing a living person or thing. This ruling gives the

**Random Question: Are there Islamic
jihadist vampires?**

This is a major question down at the ol' CIA. Most
vampires have no real allegiances except to themselves
and their coven and have no time for human philoso-
phies, political or religious. But there are individual and
groups of vampires that are willing to enter into operative
agreements with humans, for whatever reason. Intelligence
services suspect that there are various vampire collectives,
formal covens or loose groups, coming out of the Middle
East, Africa, Malaysia, and the Philippines that have contact
with jihadist groups. To what end is up to pure speculation.

But overall the vampire uprising and the ensuing fight
against them is an anti-American Islamofascist's dream
come true. What all American intelligence services fear
most is the terrorists seizing upon this period of unrest to
attempt some kind of attack, or to seek some kind of connection with vampires that aids both groups.

There is no question that there will be acts of terrorism during the vampire uprisings.

FBI (and you) all the latitude it needs to carry out "actions" against vampires: shooting them on sight.

The FBI is assembling various teams that can be dispatched to places that experience particularly large numbers of vampires or groups of exceptionally dangerous vampires. But this effort is greatly limited by national security issues connected to terrorism and the usual crime-fighting efforts of the FBI. The Bureau will also be involved in investigating vampire abductions and civilian killings. Of course, there will be many more horrors than the FBI can prevent, stop, or investigate.

The CIA

Given the Central Intelligence Agency's role in foreign intelligence gathering, its main concern during times of vampire uprising will be to identify any foreign influences on American vampirism, or track vampires infiltrating from other countries, a significant issue given the global attrac-

Vampire Fact:

The Transylvanian group the Szekelys, from which Bram Stoker's Dracula claims to descend, were, in fact, a pre-Hungarian people (or possibly a break-away Hungarian tribe) that ultimately settled in the eastern Transylvanian mountains. They became renowned as fierce and courageous protectors of this far edge of the Hungarian realm, opposing the Turks. But Stoker named his vampire after the Walachian ruler Vlad Dracula, who was not a Szekely.

Vampire Fact:

One of the most belligerent undead recorded in premodern Europe was Johannes Cuntius of Silesia, Poland, who lived sometime in the late 1500s. In his sixties, Cuntius was kicked by a horse. He briefly recovered but died soon after. A black cat scratched him the night he died. Several people reported seeing some kind of phantom in their midst before Cuntius was buried. Soon after his burial, strange sounds were heard in his former home, and outside the homes of neighbors. He reappeared in physical form and attempted to have sex with his widow and several other women in town, who reported his bad breath and b-o. He had violent confrontations with former family members and friends. He bloodied the altar cloth of the local church. He fed on the blood of all the cows until they were bled dry. Soon, the townspeople exhumed the graves of the recent dead, and found that Cuntius was the only one that hadn't decayed. His body was cut to small pieces. He never appeared again.

tiveness of the American blood feast. Already overextended by its endeavors against terrorism and in Iraq and Afghanistan, the Agency is attempting to catalog foreign covens with American connections, identify major international vampires, create intelligence sources close to those vampires, and, in a significant number of cases, make contact with the vampires themselves. A number of assets, contacts, and agents have already died in this program. The Agency has long had a small but dedicated and experienced vampire section, simply called the V-U Desk ("Vampire and Undead"), and has in the past recruited or kidnapped vampires and debriefed them extensively. Vampires were not tortured, according to most ex-Agency analysts involved in the process, as they were too valuable as assets, and are, of course, impervious to any kind of physical coercion except exsanguination and incineration. During periods of uprising in America, the Agency's role within the United States will mostly be limited to intelligence gathering and dissemination in cooperation with other security agencies, as federal laws greatly limit the CIA's ability to operate within the country. That said, agents involved in crucial overseas operations will not abandon them once their targets enter the country.

The NSA

The National Security Agency has gotten a lot of attention in recent times because they're the ones listening in on your phone calls to sex-chat lines outsourced to the Philippines. Given that many vampires have embraced digital technology, their calls will be monitored. But civilian calls will also be monitored at a much greater rate because the government will want to know what you know. Just as all those phone companies didn't get into trouble for giving the government access to everyone's phone records back in 2004 and 2005, your favorite telecom service provider will again be giving you a service—total abandonment of your privacy—you don't pay for in dollars but rights. For all practical purposes, you're going to have to assume that any given call you make or e-mail you send now, or just before, during, and after a period of vampire attack in your state is subject to federal observation via the NSA.

The CDC

The mission of the Centers for Disease Control is to protect public health by developing and applying disease prevention and control measures. CDC scientists have secretly isolated the vampire virus but have never been able to figure out much about it other than to group it in the *Lyssavirus* genus. Samples from around the world have shown a variety of strains, some much stronger than others. The CDC's goal is to develop a vaccination—something that either kills the virus or blocks its interaction with vampire hemoglo-

bin (a dynamic that still mystifies CDC virologists). Curing vampires of vampirism is not on the CDC's priority list. That is simply too difficult a task. The Center's doctors and scientists believe that focusing on the living is a much better approach, and have developed some ideas about how to limit the transference of the virus and how to combat the transforming effects of the vampire hemoglobin-virus interaction (as discussed in chapter 1).

During periods of vampire attack, the CDC will take as many samples of vampire and victim blood as possible, in an attempt to identify the strains of the virus in the United States, study the capabilities of vampire hemoglobin, continually refine the science behind limiting the disease's effects, and, hopefully, eventually find a way to neutralize it. Many university and college medical labs will be involved with the CDC in this effort, and you can bet that Big Pharma is hustling right along, too. Imagine the profits of the first effective vampirism antibiotic.

The Military

Widespread vampire uprisings necessitate an extensive police action combined with a well-coordinated counterattacking force on the ground, with pin-point support from the air. In other words, tanks, large air strikes, ballistic missiles, and artillery do not have a role, because destroying ourselves to save ourselves doesn't usually work.

Wrung-out, tired, and overextended by warfare in Afghanistan, Iraq, and elsewhere, the most useful forces of the Army, Navy, Marines, and Air Force will have a tough time mounting the coordinated operations needed to detect and destroy the undead. Marines, navy personnel, and SEALs will have roles to play along the coasts and in riverine situations. Rangers, Marines, SEALs, and Special Forces will deploy inland. Aircraft especially useful for counterattack, mainly special-ops choppers, reconnaissance drones, and various spy planes, will come into play extensively. But in general, military forces will be fighting a guerilla war.

Surviving the Bureaucrats with Guns

In some places, Americans will have to interact frequently with various badge-toting bureaucrats or military honchos. Post-9/11 laws allow the military to control the civilian population in times of national emergency, so you'll be beholden to all of them: local and state cops, FBI agents, and commanding military officers. *Doing what they say isn't an option, but playing off their needs and wants is*. To do so, you need to tune in to each.

The Military: Wants civilians to stay out of the way or move to where the officers tell them to go. Wants to use your big backyard as a heliport. Wants a string of tactical victories leading up to overall victory. *Your part:* Be nice to frontline

Vampire Fact:

Probably the two most infamous "government" officials directly connected to vampirism in Western civilization are the Walachian leaders Vlad Dracul (1390–1447) and his son, Vlad Dracula (1431–76). Vlad Dracul took the throne of Walachia (a portion of modern-day Romania) in 1437 and entered into a hazardous pact with the Turks, making himself an enemy of the Hungarians and ruling Romanians, the boyars. Hungarian forces murdered him in 1447, with Romanian help. Vlad Dracula (meaning "son of Dracul") managed to succeed his father to the throne of Walachia in 1456 after forming a crafty alliance with the Hungarians. In 1459, he took revenge against the boyars for his father's murder, impaling many on stakes and forcing many others into slave labor to build a fortress on the Arges River, a structure later known as Castle Dracula. Vlad Dracula committed countless acts of totalitarian brutality across Romania, earning him the bloody title *Tepes*, "The Impaler," until his assassination in 1476.

soldiers or marines. Find out who the sergeants and captains are. Offer information (including what you know about other federal agencies) in exchange for assurances the armed forces will try to keep themselves from driving a Bradley Fighting Vehicle through your garage. Make sure they know the location of your house and who you are.

The FBI: Wants to know everything about everyone. Wants you to cooperate. Wants to capture vampires alive. *Your part*: While the FBI won't have time to pay too much attention to regular law enforcement during the vampire uprising, if they take an interest in you, you'll get the full treatment. So the best thing to do if approached by the FBI is satisfy them, either by demonstrating that you're a complete ignoramus and not worth their time, or by tossing up whatever you know about the military snooping around and seemingly nefarious behavior by local law enforcement. If the feds start asking questions about your neighbors ("Has Mr. Flanders ever talked about drinking blood, even casually?") you've got to make a difficult choice. Remember, your neighbor's your neighbor, while the FBI is not particularly concerned with helping you. Of course, if your neighbor is a real idiot who's suing you because he fell into your vampire tiger trap, you can get rid of both him and the feds with a simple nod of your head.

The cops: Want to make enough arrests to stay on top of promotions. Want less paperwork. Want to go home alive at the end of their shift. *Your part:* When this whole bloodsucking

Inquisitive
FBI Agent

wackiness is over, and the feds and army guys turn the car around, you'll still have the cops. Getting to know your local law enforcement officers by face and name is always a good idea, and if you can tip them off to any worthwhile information during the uprising, they'll appreciate it. Even if the police in your township are real meatheads, staying on their good side is ideal, at least during the vampire uprising.

Of course, plenty of local police will take it upon themselves to pull a Gary Cooper and try to deputize a bunch of civilians to go vampire hunting. State laws vary on this, but for the most part you can refuse deputization and be entirely within your rights. You'll have to weigh the impact of joining or not joining local defense groups, and, indeed, you might affect your social standing depending upon your decision. Tough call.

Also note: The military will extensively employ mercenaries in places where it cannot effectively deploy its own troops. These "military contractors" will be paid (by us, really) to handle security and vampire-hunting roles, and will for the most part consider themselves tantamount to the Army—meaning that they expect you, the civilian, to do what they say. You don't have to from a legal standpoint, because they do not carry the same authority as actual military officers, but they will always be better armed than you.

Chapter 6

As the Blood Gushes . . .

So, here you are: You spend your days working at your job as much as you can, where your supervisors shout at employees about productivity while employees shout back about security. Somebody has to be home to meet the kids when they get off the school bus or collect them at a neighbor's house on the way home. Rush hour is a free-for-all as everyone scrambles to get home with at least an hour of daylight left to check on the home defenses, warning systems, and vampire traps. Then, just before the sun disappears, the locks are locked, the gear comes out, and everyone hunkers down in their stations to make calls and check e-mails. Recreation is sporadic. Weekends are spent catching up on sleep and burning dead vampires. *And don't forget the exciting part: actually shooting the bloodsuckers.*

Your new, exhausting lifestyle is going to last anywhere from a month to an entire season, and possibly longer. America will be a different place for a while, what with everyone changing their habits, fearing vampiric transformation, and getting generally more belligerent. No one's going to really give a damn about the rest of the world for a while (and the rest of the world will be grateful). But we're going to have to cope effectively with ourselves, and that will be an added challenge.

The Human Threat

Being able to trust someone, or determine quickly that you can't trust someone, will be an essential part of your surviv-

Vampire Fact:

In what might be the most extraordinary discovery of delayed vampirism, an Austrian military inquiry into several cases of possible undead activity in the 1720s found credible evidence suggesting that three unrelated, deceased men had reappeared and killed family members ten, sixteen, and thirty years respectively after each had died. Two of these vampires were cremated; the third had a long nail driven through his skull and was reburied. None arose or attacked again.

ing the whole damn fracas. So a little insight into American's reactions to continually marauding vampires will help you clarify your thinking for future moments of split-second decision making.

Differing Points of View About the Vampire Uprising

Beliefs about the causes of the uprising and what it all means will vary greatly. But sometimes you have to judge someone on basic opinions alone. Some possible viewpoints:

This is worse than the Civil War and 9/11 combined. This might strike you as pure hyperbole or ironic realism, but you'll have to decide which, because having realistic people around is a good idea, but you don't want strategic hypochondriacs or those wackos who've read every book about Nostradamus (unless they're excellent with a shotgun and a spotlight, and then you might be willing to banter all night about prophesy and black helicopters).

God is punishing us, and only when we rid ourselves of sin will we repel the bloodsucking hordes. Religious reactions to the vampires will run the gamut and will often be loud, strained, and terrifically didactic. However, faith-based anti-vampire forces will be well organized and highly motivated. Whether you think a Judeo-Christian or Islamic or any kind of god is punishing you or testing you is something you'll have to figure out on your own, but you cannot undervalue the dedication and courage of religious fighters. They're good to have around. But eventually some of them will ask you what you believe and if you're "with them," and this could be a troubling moment for the Jewish person asked by a Pentecostal, or a lapsed Unitarian faced down by a bunch of armed Catholic deacons (can Unitarians actually lapse?).

This is a huge leap of evolution, and we might actually have no choice but to become vampires. *Don't* give this person a firearm, at least not until you beat this silly defeatist thinking out of him with a tennis racket and he finally says, "OK, OK, this isn't biologically inevitable." Start this person out with simple chores and move him up to spotlighter, and only when you have witnessed that an attacking vampire has sufficiently scared the bejesus out of him should you ask, "Do you think you can defend yourself now, instead of embracing life as a bipedal leech?"

The government knew this was going to happen and they're going to save all the rich people and let the rest of us die. That's not too crazy, actually, because rich folks are going to have the means to protect themselves very well. But how did all those rich people get rich? Off of the hard work and taxes of the rest of us, so they're not going to let the labor force die (much). Is it possible some towns and cities won't get the military support other places will enjoy? Definitely yes. Demographics are a bitch sometimes.

Are There " Black" Vampires, "White" Vampires, "Latino" Vampires, Etc.?

As a physiological fact, race doesn't much survive vampirism; the anatomical and genetic traits that might identify a person as being of one race or another can get significantly blurred through the transformation from human to vampire. Vampires don't have any kind of "uniform" skin color, and one and all are often thought of as being a race unto themselves.

But whatever human memory a vampire might possess will be greatly influenced by the culture and socialization of that former person. The recently transformed vampire will naturally seek out other newly transformed vampires that she or he might know from human life (often family members attacked at the same time). Older vampires often belong to regional covens or groups that are composed of the undead that once came from specific ethnicities or sects. Ultimately, a vampire would think of itself as belonging to a specific coven or sect that might have a collective human memory influenced by race, among many other things, but it will consider itself a vampire first, and then a member of a specific vampire association. It will think little beyond that about group identity.

So you might call a bloodsucker the "Irish vampire" or "Puerto Rican vampire" by way of identifying origin and (arbitrary) identifying traits, but referring to the same one as a "Caucasian vampire" or "Latino vampire" respectively is inaccurate.

Crime and Cultural Clashes During the Uprising

Using the vampire chaos as cover, thousands of professional criminals will go to work. They will pose as police, members of the military, religious fighters, or mercenaries, or they will try to pass themselves off as regular Americans trying to resist the vampires. Their objectives are the same as usual: robbery, larceny, rape, extortion, murder, and identity theft. They will, however, face an army of armed private citizens. This will give some of them pause, and others will simply call upon every criminal talent they have. Clearly, criminals who work during daylight hours will pose fewer troubles than the beings you face at night, while those human criminals who come in the night are either extremely skilled, extremely crazy, or both, and are asking for it.

As a veteran vampire hunter once said, "Don't trust vampires, and trust people less."

As for cultural upheavals, social interactions will be greatly curtailed while the vampire horde is on the move, so whatever upheavals that might occur will happen mostly online. Wars of words, both rhetorical and truly threatening, will rage in thousands of chat rooms and blogs. Who's suffering the most? Who's resisting the most? Who should be in charge of the country? Who owes whom for fighting against

Vampire Fact:
Ancient Romans believed in a creature of significant vampire traits, the *strix,* although this entity was more like a witch than the undead. The *strix*, like many other vampire-like beings, preyed upon infants, drinking their blood.

the vampires? The lines for the post-uprising culture wars will be drawn in cyberspace, and both the vampires and the government will closely monitor all of this spew.

But isolated actual clashes and protests will occur during the rampant vampire period. Some cities and towns will see extended periods of little vampire activity, leaving the populace rested but restless and eager to register their complaints on foot, in groups. Expect demonstrations against the vampires themselves, as well as protests about government abuses of power, military screwups, police heavy-handedness, and perceived disparities in distribution of anti-vampire funding. To the extent that there will be some vampires arriving from overseas, there will be protests demanding better border control.

Whether you participate in a protest has everything to do with how much time and energy you've got. In regular times, those things are usually at a premium. When you're trying to fortify and defend your home and help your neighborhood watch keep tabs on vampires you've ID'd as local bloodsuckers, protests will probably be the last thing on your mind. However, maintaining the institutions that make us the United States of America is part of our political survival.

Vampires and Sexuality

Ancient demonic figures closely associated with vampirism, the male incubus and the female succubus, had definite sexual natures. The incubus demon steals upon a sleeping woman and rapes her, while the succubus sexually saps a man in his sleep. Neither demonic being, however, drank the blood of its victims.

For vampires, sex with humans is a secondary pleasure to feasting, but it can be part of the attack. Both male and female victims of attacking and feeding vampires report that the powerfully hypnotic gaze and voice of the vampire greatly hindered their physical ability to fight back. Female vampires have the particular ability to suspend their male victim's sense of fear to create a necessary physical reaction, though feeding female vampires do not always ravage their male or female victims. The same goes for male vampires: They might be particularly keen on a certain kind of victim, but this interest is all about feasting from that victim, and not raping him or her.

Vampire Fact:

The case of the Serbian vampire Peter Plogojowitz began with his death in 1728. Three nights after his death, he went to his house and asked his son for food, and the son gave him some. He repeated this two nights later, and his son refused him. Family members found the son dead the next day. Over the next week, nine villagers who reported having dreams of being bitten on the neck by Plogojowitz all died of exhaustion due to blood loss. Townspeople summoned an Austrian military commander, who ordered Plogojowitz exhumed. Plogojowitz's body appeared alive, and he had blood smeared around the his mouth. The commander wasted no time and had a stake driven through Plogojowitz's heart and the body cremated.

Among themselves, vampires will engage in sexual activity during feasts, but their sexual endeavors are powered by their pleasure and energy in consuming blood. Female vampires cannot conceive.

Extralegal and Psychological Issues

As the vampire attacks wear on, you're going to find yourself willing to take greater risks as a citizen than ever before, for the sake of your survival. This isn't about whether you're willing to venture out at night as part of a hunter team—this has more to do with your willingness to bend or break laws and push the limits of human-to-human interaction when the chips are down.

The main factor in this is how you deal with the lawlessness of other Americans, as the police, National Guard, and select military units are distracted by the hunting and killing of vampires. Driven by fear, desperation, or paranoia, some people will try to steal from you, while on other occasions you might face violent people. Professional criminals will seek to fill voids of law enforcement with fraud and racketeering ("Looks like you could use some vampire protection, buddy—know what I mean?"), smuggling and drug production, and illegal arms sales.

How you react when faced with these human elements will have a large impact on your overall survival. Do you deal

Delirium from vampire hunting sets in

Random Question: My ex-girlfriend's new boyfriend isn't a vampire, but I'm paying a vampire to turn him into one so I can shoot him. Is this wrong?

That's pretty stone cold, but don't think you're the first person to come up with this idea. "Contract vampirism," as it is called, will be a widespread and easy way to camouflage humans' murderous intentions. The dangerous part is making contact with a vampire to arrange the "hit," but there will be numerous middlemen that can be contacted through the black market to have such a contract created.

Is this immoral? You bet. Is it low-down dirty? Indeed. Is her new boyfriend a total scumbag man-ho who's got it coming? *Your call.*

with such people as if they were vampires, knowing that you can get away with it? If you feel your life is in danger, you might just have to.

Human Psychological Reaction to Waves of Vampire Attacks

No matter how tight a grip you might have on your sanity before the uprisings, when these troubles are over, it will be loosened quite a bit. A major problem for a lot of people will be the disruption in the production, distribution, and retail availability of many mental-health medications. But bipolar or not, you will have to find a way to keep things together in your head so that you don't end up losing a lot of blood. So be aware ahead of time of the various acute reactions you might have to the stresses of this crisis:

Overwhelming fear and panic

A little fear is natural and keeps you on your toes. Debilitating fear is no good. The thing to do when this happens is to talk to someone and use the dialogue to identify why your fear is so extreme and how to start reducing it bit by bit. You're not going to find random psychotherapists behind every barred door, however, but you need to find some way to exercise your problem and break it down into workable portions. Develop a few mantras: "America will endure." "I will survive." "Vampires can be stopped." "I'm taking charge of my situation." This sounds hokey, but your home-made Klonopin won't do any better.

Extreme, uncontrollable aggression

Your sense of the threat to your life and person coupled with the necessity of killing vampires can unleash long pent-up feelings of rage, powerlessness, and interest in violence for violence's sake. People who have such undiagnosed problems can pose serious danger to themselves, family members, team members, and really anyone who comes to the door. They usually can't fix themselves on their own, and for safety's sake, you or someone else is going to have to put this person in as neutral a situation as possible: no weapons, minimal responsibilities, and constant observation. None of that will be easy as vampire attacks peak in your area.

Vampiric delusions and vampire-related paranoia

Some people will begin to believe they have been turned into vampires or bitten by vampires when they actually have not. This can become a pretty powerful delusion, and only through steady dissuasion by friends and family members can the person be led step by logical step back to the reality of his or her personal state. Other people will begin to see vampires everywhere—out every window, scratching at the basement door, and even standing in the room with them. Such paranoiacs can be dangerous and need to be disarmed, if necessary, and calmed as thoroughly as possible. Beyond that, such people need to be paired with healthy, rational people who can provide a model for regaining clear, accurate perceptions.

Debilitating cognitive dissonance

The random and circular nature of the vampire uprising—attacks, then lulls, then attacks again, coupled with the transformation of former friends into bloodsuckers—will cause even the most sound-minded strategist to begin to fail at the $2 + 2 = 4$ logic that human brains rely on. Expecting the unexpected is a sensible response, but extended periods of nonsensical events leads to brain freeze, because no one fact can be built upon another; necessary links and consistencies of narrative aren't available. Herein is the source of myth-making: trying to explain the inexplicable so that human beings can function. So it doesn't hurt to mythologize small parts of what you're doing—that is, come up with your own self-to-self marketing angle on troublesome parts of your situation that lets you stay on task. Just be honest later about what you've ignored or glossed over.

Desire for transformation

Some people who have long harbored sympathy for, or sexual interests in vampires and vampirism will seek literally to embrace the undead and become vampires themselves. Most Americans will be able to see the insanity of this and put aside their fantasies. Others, however, will have to be watched and possibly restrained. Someone who seeks to venture out at night or attempts to create entryways into a secured home must be foiled for everyone's safety.

Dealing with the Stresses of Killing

Successful survival will sometimes mean killing vampires. And while many of these creatures will seem so repellent and frightful that killing them will be a psychological relief, other times the shooters of your team or family will wonder whether they're actually killing people who seem just a little strange. And a lot of shooting will be stressful, no matter what. Here are ways to cope:

Cooling off after a vampire killing: Shooting a vampire is always an ugly and terrifying event. The shooter team might express nervous excitement, awkward bravado, or vomiting afterward. All of these are stress reactions. Shooter teams should be given food and water, a chance to rest, and someone to talk to about what happened—not only for the sake of tactical self-education, but also to work the events into a story that can be handled emotionally. Rewards are also a good idea, as they give the team members a sense that they acted rightly.

Itchy trigger finger: If you sense that you are pumped up and ready to start blasting the minute you look out your window, you need to do some relaxation exercises and perhaps have a talk with yourself about fire discipline. Working through a series of tactical positive visualizations is another good way to settle the nerves and get your game face on rather than just staying jumpy.

Vampire Fact:

The American staging of the play *Dracula* opened in New York in 1927, with Hungarian actor Béla Lugosi as the title character, while the first full-length vampire feature film, *London After Midnight*, premiered the same year, starring Lon Chaney. Lugosi went on to star in the 1931 American film version of *Dracula*. Three previous attempts at a cinematic interpretation of the novel had already been made: by Russian filmmakers in 1920 (no copy of that film survives), by Hungarian filmmakers in 1921, and by the German makers of *Nosferatu* in 1922, which was not authorized by the Bram Stoker estate; most copies of *Nosferatu* were destroyed as a result of the ensuing rights dispute, but one copy did survive and became available in 1984.

Team discipline after a tough night: The day after an active night of vampire sightings and shootings is the right time for the family or team leader to praise the team and analyze what went right and wrong. Take this time to air worries and fears that result from having seen so many vampires so close, and then develop new tactics or spot remedies for dealing with these troubles as a team. And get as much rest as possible.

Learning to enjoy successful survival: Some people will gloat over dead vampires. Others will feel a weird remorse. You might feel a kind of savagery about what you are doing, but you should understand that noble, righteous savagery is not a bad thing. Do not have a second thought about being glad you're still alive.

Resisting Celebrity Vampires

The obsession with celebrity in this country verges on psychosis. And there are five main sources of celebrity and celebrities: L.A., Las Vegas, New York, Miami, and Washington, D.C. So you shouldn't be surprised to learn that a number of VIPs are actually "VIVs." These "Very Important Vampires," or cele-vamps, have used the camouflage and privilege of celebrity and political power to insert themselves into American pop culture and public life—no easy task, certainly, but one made easier by our cultural willingness to let ourselves be dazzled by airbrushed hacks, louts, and frauds. As most of these celebrity leeches are maniacally egotistical, they will be offended, outraged, and put on the defensive by the uprising hordes of "common" vampires, and will present the American human population a unique set of problems.

How to Tell Who's a Cele-Vamp

There are three essential clues to identify cele-vamps:

1. They never rise above the B-list: Staying at the B-list or, even better, C-list level of celebrity allows the cele-vamp to maintain all the necessary eccentricities of life as a "serious" actor (avoids the sun due to strange skin condition; enjoys special "macro

All the Best!

liquid diet"), while commanding some respect for notable roles in small-budget or indie films that go nowhere.

2. They manage to get into any party anywhere: Perhaps you've witnessed some C-lister who somehow always rubs elbows with the A-list crowd, and no one really remembers her or is sure about her name ("Maybe she's someone's life coach?"). She's always very well behaved and well spoken, and yet she always knows someone who can get anything for you at any hour: serious drugs, a custom chopper, a machine gun, or a donkey.

3. They occasionally disappear from the industry and the scene: No one will notice that these people have been gone for a year until one of them pops up in yet another indie film. They change agents and publicists frequently, yet somehow always manage to have a great rep agency and get work when they want it.

You might think a major clue as to who is a cele-vamp is whether she or he eats. But all celebrities are either not eating anything, eating a very strict diet, or eating everything edible in L.A. (including other celebrities). Plus, just about any celebrity can get away with not ever being seen eating by saying, when questioned about it, "I've got to stay in shape for my next role."

Ignoring the Cele-Vamp Hype

During the uprising, certain cele-vamps will be identified. Other, foreign vampires of prominence will also become known by name. And among the many strange things that will happen during this crisis, these creatures will somehow derive heightened social status from their identity as vampires. They'll be the ultimate bad boys or bad girls who command attention, respect, and even worship. They will be surrounded by members of their coven, human and vampire acolytes, and the ever-present bloodsucker paparazzi—an entire contingent of American media dedicated to covering the hottest names and faces of the vampire world.

You will see all this lunacy and folderol on television and in your magazines. Don't waste any energy despising it. Simply ignore it, while making a mental note that you'd shoot any vampire, celebrity or not, if they tried to get into your home.

A rat is a rat. A roach is a roach. And a bloodsucker is a bloodsucker even if repped by the William Morris Agency or ICM.

Evading the Cele-Vamp

If you're at a social gathering—an Oscar party, a coming-out party, a Bar Mitzvah—and you ID a cele-vamp (an ID you'd have to base on previously assembled data, of course), then evade this vampire at all costs:

Do not talk to the cele-vamp's publicist. If you find your-self engaged in a very chatty, one-sided conversation with someone, often a very well-dressed young woman, who sounds like she knows everyone, ask her if she's a publicist. If so, for whom. If this woman names the vampire, grab your jacket pocket and say suddenly, "Oh, my, that's my phone—it's my agent. I have to take this. Sorry," and get the hell away from her.

Don't fall in with the cele-vamp's friends. Say you find yourself in the back of a club with a bunch of pretty cool people—good-looking men and women. Before you start to think about your chances of not going home alone *again*, ask a few of them if they know the vampire. They might recognize the bloodsucker but don't know him—this is good. But if they say, "Oh, yeah, he's our best bud—he in-vited us here," politely nod, make some small talk, and slip away at the first chance you get, or you're going to find yourself among these people, hanging by your feet, while a small coven of C-list cele-vamps drinks from tubes inserted in your neck.

Skip the after party. Sure, the after party is where all the real deals get made, all the really sexy stuff happens, and the real scene is going down. But if there's anyplace that a cele-vamp will strike, it's the after party at the loft downtown. You won't even know it's the cele-vamp's loft—there's just a bunch of people going there, and you go with them, and when you get there there's a vampire standing in the middle of the room in a gorgeous, deathly white Stella McCartney dress and you know she can smell your blood.

> **Vampire Fact:**
> As the Eastern Orthodox Church came to rule Russian religious life, vampirism became closely tied to heresy. A person who broke with church doctrine, especially one that had become involved with sorcery, could easily come back as a vampire after death. The *eretik* ("heretic") used an evil eye to draw victims to their fate. An *eretik* could be killed by cremation or with an aspen stake driven through its heart.

Resisting Political Vampires

Political vampires are even more pernicious and widespread than celebrity vampires. They can also hold you in a double bind of legal hassle and blood predation. The IRS already wants enough from you without your having to face an auditor who shows up at twilight. But there are precautions you can take.

Identifying Political Vampires

Politico-vamps take much greater pains than cele-vamps to conceal themselves because they seek to gain power without direct participation in the political process (elected officials cannot avoid the sun entirely). Such bloodsuckers are almost always consultants, lobbyists, and strategists, or act to impersonate actual politicians during the nighttime hours. No vampire could run for or hold public office—that's just not possible or practical. But one can easily remain in the shadows behind major campaigns. Some basic characteristics:

Nocturnal deal making: Big decisions and deals are often made in America's power centers well after dark. The politico-vamp always has territory staked out at the best restaurants, swankiest bars, and hottest after-hours clubs to get legislators, commissioners, and directors to sit down, cut through the BS, and make a deal happen.

Respected and liked, but not well-known: Vampires hiding in political careers tend to treat their staffs well but don't make friends of them. The bloodsucker makes the most of the political hierarchy to keep subordinate and superior staff members at just the right distance.

Sticklers for procedure: Adhering to structure and method gives the political vampire camouflage and a way of demonstrating honesty and uprightness when under scrutiny. Every necessary form must be filled out with the proper number of copies made.

Senior or valued enough to set own hours: This is probably the most crucial trait: the bureaucrat that's never in the office during daylight working hours. This is terrifically difficult to pull off and calls for an efficient support staff and forgiving superiors. But thanks to the terrifically complicated bureaucratic systems of the Clinton years, the Bush-2 years, and the Iraq War, wholly irregular hours and work habits are now commonplace among various agencies. Bottom line: If, after numerous requests, you still haven't met a political operative during daylight hours, you might be lobbying the undead.

If You Kill a Celebrity Vampire

Imagine this conversation taking place in your living room after you blast a bloodsucker:

Friend:	Jeez, that was close. Nice shot.
You:	I'm getting better. Hey, look at this leech. You recognize him?
Friend:	He looks like that guy from . . . what's that show?
You:	Oh, yeah, that show with the cool cars.
Friend:	Damn—it is him. This guy was Pam Anderson's fourth husband. It was in all the papers.
You:	Oh . . . shit.

Killing a well-known vampire can have some serious consequences. This is a bloodsucker that probably had living and undead friends who will be quite enraged that he's dead. If he belonged to a powerful coven, there's a chance they might come looking for vengeance. So get ready for some quick and quiet work.

Shoot, Burn, and Shovel

Out west, there's an old expression: "Shoot, shovel, and shut up." This has been applied to all sorts of things: crazed vagrants, endangered species, railroad bankers. In your case, if you shoot and kill a vampire who you think is recognizable, behead, incinerate, and bury the ashes of said bloodsucker as quickly as you can in as remote a place as you can find.

Shut Up

You're an upstanding member of your neighborhood watch and vampire patrol? Fine, very good. You're supposed to log and report every bloodsucker you or your team kills? OK, righto. And you shot a vampire last night that looked a lot like that guy from Maroon 5? No . . . no you didn't. You shot nothing last night. Dull night. Quiet.

Deny, Deny, Deny, and Issue Counteraccusations

Somehow a rumor starts that you and your lovely Remington ventilated a major indie-film director who made that picture about the beautifully comic, quirkily dysfunctional rich family in Brooklyn. What do you do? Say nothing until asked. And when asked, state just once these three very clear denials: "I don't know anything about that. I don't know who committed the shooting. I don't even know if it actually occurred." Then declare that the people who want to connect you to the shooting are vampires themselves who are trying to smear a good, red-blooded living American and should be investigated.

Fighting Loose Lips

Obviously, if someone in your family or team knows you killed a cele-vamp, you're going to have to rely on that person to keep quiet. The more people who know, the greater your risk. Problems will emerge when:

1. Suspicions arise about the cele-vamp when he or she disappears (for good).
2. Other vampires float rumors and innuendo, some of which will be highly accurate, putting the dead cele-vamp in your neighborhood and possibly near your house.
3. Editors from the gossip rags start calling and offering money for anyone who has information about the guy from Maroon 5 who's missing (yeah, really—they're *actually looking* for him).

Cleaning Up the Cele-vamp

As soon as you ID a cele-vamp, decapitate the body and secure the head in burnable material—burlap, a backpack, or an old blanket—and then a plastic bag. Stash it away secretly and let no one else see it. Set up a cremation the following day and start burning the head as quickly as you can. If you've other undead bodies to burn, mix them in with the cele-vamp.

Don't worry much about any blood or tissue spatter. Vampire blood/DNA can't be traced to the original human victim, and most likely the cele-vamp has never had its human DNA taken on record. Just clean up the blood when you can.

A Little PR Never Hurts

Without bravado, and certainly without asking directly for anything in return, you might quietly show friends videos or still photos of non-cele-vamp kills (of bloodsuckers that can't be ID'd in the photo, either), just to let everyone know you're doing your part. You break a dozen kills before the end of a season, and people will start calling you "Ace." What you want is for your neighbors and friends to hold you in esteem and be wiling to defend you if accused of cele-vamp shooting. They're not going to give a damn if you blasted vampire Erik Estrada unless they're hard-core *CHiPs* fans, and even then . . .

But they will give a damn if you face possible trouble for something that they think shouldn't matter when everyone is struggling to stay alive.

When Does It End?

The tricky thing about a mass vampire attack is that while it has a pretty clear beginning, it has a long and muddled middle and a not-so-clear ending. Say, for example, vampires start taking victims in Washington, D.C. They take as much blood in the city as they want, and then some of them move on to Alexandria and other suburbs, or northward into rural Maryland. A number of them get killed in the city or during their haunts of the suburban and rural areas, and the remainder revert to a quiet, careful predatory existence and remain in the shadows for many months to come.

Is that an ending?

Yes, in terms of vampires, it is something of an ending, however sketchy. After several weeks of steadily fighting off and/or killing several vampires per week, you might observe just a few vampires roaming in the distance at night, and then see none for many successive nights. Your network will report few sightings and even fewer attempted attacks. Most new vampires will have died due to inexperience and buckshot; only about 10 percent of the brand-new American vampire population will survive past its first year. They will eventually either find residency in America, or roam the earth.

Local vampire populations in some areas could remain strong even after periods of regular attack end. Covens of bloodsuckers in high-nutrient, low-defense areas might hang on a long time. This period will have its own specific troubles related to your attempts to collect better intelligence about the crisis itself and the state of your neighbor-

Random Question: What's the legal status of an American turned into a vampire, but who has pledged to not attack humans or drink human blood? (He's a brother Mason and I trust him.)

That's a good question. Many Americans will call for death for all vampires, regardless of any pledges of peaceable behavior. Federal authorities will have to decide on a procedure for American citizens who become vampirized but refuse to live the vampire lifestyle. Many lawmakers and religious leaders will want at least some kind of imprisonment for those who become vampires. But scientists, academics, and many other Americans will want to have in place some method for accepting nonviolent vampires, especially those who not so long ago were human members of our families.

But, at the end stage of the uprising, many newly transformed American vampires will have no choice but to go into hiding. Those that are members of powerful organizations, such as your Masonic lodge, or the military, might be able to find friends who will hide and protect them. Others will simply have to rely on their new survival skills and hover at the edges of civilization, living off animals, until they have an opportunity to find shelter among humans.

The nonviolent vampire should posses a number of documents, in case he needs to prove who he once was:

Driver's license, passport, birth certificate, and Social Security card: These things will prove a former human existence; the birth certificate and Social Security card are the most crucial.

Affidavits from witnesses: Those who saw someone attacked by a vampire, or found the person after an attack and noted the transformation into vampirism, should write out legal statements saying that the person in question was attacked and transformed against his or her will.

Written pledge of nonviolence: While it might not convince many people, a vampire who writes and signs a pledge of living a nonviolent existence has at least made an official declaration, one to which he must conform if the rest of his legal status and survival are to work out.

hood. You will also run into the unusual and dangerous problems of three distinct fighting entities—civilian, intelligence, and military—trying to pull back from full combat mode. So while you might be able to take down some of the fortifications of your home, and possibly move about at night, you're going to have to remain on alert as America brings itself back on line.

The last thing you want is false hope that life might be returning to "normal" and that you might actually hold on to your complete blood volume. When vampire attacks slacken, you'll need to rely on your communication and intelligence networks just as much as you did during the worst times.

Continue to Tally Vampire Sightings and Attacks

With the necessary exclusions for cele-vamp killings, keep your log of events, attacks, and vampire sightings and killings up to date. You might throw all this data into your computer and have it calculate the trends, if you're a vampi-geek. Note any anomalies: new, strange-looking, or emaciated vampires, new signs of group movement, or bodies of vampires that you find during the day that you did not slay yourself. As the active period of the uprising subsides, vampires out to settle turf wars with other vampires will finish their business. While most vampire-on-vampire violence leaves little in the way of remains, sometimes a vampire will leave the body of a rival as a message to others in the area.

Continue to Communicate Regularly with Your Contacts

The phone calls, e-mails, letters, video conferencing, and face-to-face meetings should remain on schedule. Ask your network for any statistics they can provide, and compare those to yours. Attempt to work up data for as large an area as possible, and look for sections of your neighborhood or county that are witnessing regular and significant vampire movement with low attack numbers. If you reach a point where you haven't had a sighting of a vampire in over two weeks, and few signs of vampire movement are found, the main attack phase in your area is most likely over. Plot this information on your data map and compare it to the data from the height of the uprising. Specifically, if you're finding that you and your neighbors are registering no sightings or encounters at all in previous hot spots, *your situation is looking up.*

Work with Your Police, Military, and Black Market Contacts

No matter how disgruntled you might have become with police methods, military bull-in-a-China-shop mistakes, or the skeeviness of some of your black-market dealings (where else were you going to find *all* of the *Xena: Warrior Princess* DVDs?), you should have exploited them as much as you could as sources of information during the main period of vampire combat, and you should continue to seek opinions whenever you can. You'll have to filter a ton of rumors to get a few worthy nuggets of fact, but even rumor is worth knowing, as you'll learn about the mindset of those passing along rumors sincerely or sarcastically.

Of particular note: If the military presence in your area suddenly drops off to nothing, that's usually a good sign, but don't get too excited. The costs of moving various Marine Corps and Special Forces units all around the country to zap the leeches are going to seriously mount up. Budgets and regional strategies will come into play. Your area might no longer be so lousy with bloodsuckers that the digiflage gang decides to go hunting elsewhere, but you, American citizen, can be expected to continue to fight for yourself.

Vampire Fact:

A Chinese person who died violently, or who committed suicide, or died by improper burial could become a vampire called a *chiang-shih*, a vicious bloodsucker that ambushed victims and often dismembered and decapitated them, and raped female victims. These vampires sometimes had a greenish glow about their bodies, and long fingernails and fangs. After gaining strength by drinking blood, the *chaing-shih* would grow long white hair and, reportedly, develop the ability to fly, while others were said to sometimes be able to transform into wolves. In this powerful form, only a bullet or fire could destroy the *chiang-shih*.

Radio, TV, and Internet

Monitor all media as best you can, assuming the power has not been off for so long that Internet and digital cable service have been curtailed. You might have to hook up the rabbit ears or the old roof aerial to get any reception. At this point of the crisis, the news services should have gotten their act together, and if they have any sense of responsibility, they will report the most relevant information via the most easily broadcast media available—radio and "free TV." Getting timely local news in smaller markets and rural areas will be tough, as ever, and your conversations at the diner, gas station, or grain silos might continue to do just fine.

Dangers of the Final Stages

The structural damage, psychological damage, loss of life and livelihood, and echoes of violence of this intense period are going to create endless malfunction and dysfunction as Americans slowly get back to having their country to themselves again. This will be like cleaning up after some kind of wave of odd tornados. Expect massive weirdness, so don't put the shotgun away yet (er . . . you probably don't ever want to really put it away where you can't get it, y' know?).

Humans Who Won't Quit

Because they're suffering a mental illness, or because they're natural paranoiacs, or because they've actually enjoyed themselves, some Americans who have killed their fair share of vampires will refuse to accept general opinions that vampire numbers are visibly waning. They will not remove the fortifications from their homes, cabins, or trailers, and they will continue to stay armed, their shotgun slung over their shoulders, a big-bore revolver on their hip. *In many ways, they can't be blamed.* Theirs is a meaningful, even successful, lifestyle they've carved out for themselves. And what's to say that the country isn't going to fall apart socially? Or by its weakened state invite (another) attack by foreign *humans*? But you're going to have to assess your local survivalist-type and judge whether you can deal with him at all or just keep a very polite distance. Determine which group this person falls into:

The Stay-the-Courser: This guy was smart and reliable during the uprising period, and says he has no plans to change his lifestyle until he is satisfied no vampires live in his home state (and if this is West Virginia, he's damn serious about that). He continues to operate local day- and nighttime vampire hunts and maintains traps on his property. The uprising won't be over for him for two or three years. But in general, this fellow is fine. Keep up with him as you did during the uprising, though he might lose a bit of faith in you when you say you can't go vampire hunting every weekend anymore.

The Smoke-'Em-Outer: This one thinks there are still many lingering vampires (quite possible) and demands that every nook, cranny, barn, drainpipe, patch of woods, warehouse, and sewer in the country must be searched and the vampires killed, impaled, and burned in public. She then calls for vampire-virus testing for all Americans and seeks ways to get legislation about this introduced at the state level; such legislation would call for a quarantine of those who test positive. She also demands zero immigration for five years. This gal is going to be a little difficult to deal with, given the various social constructs necessary to get America running again. Try to work with people like this on a case-by-case basis, but don't expect much.

The Secessionist: This person goes off the grid, proclaiming his own province within the borders of his property line or domicile. The laws of the county, state, and country do not apply within that province. If you knew this person before or during the chaos and had some liking for him, you might be able to maintain contact (if you so desire), but be cautious, as all other people will be outsiders to this person, and you've no idea what kind of paranoia might be building in this tiny, double-wide nation of his.

The Martial-Law-and-Order Guy: Calls for a militarized America and seeks to join the military or create his own militia allied with the Department of Defense. Wants all worthy American adults drafted and given rank and duties within some kind of military organization. Demands unilateral hunting and destruction of vampires anywhere in the world. This type is going to be a little difficult to listen to after awhile, but definitely keep an eye on him. Don't be surprised when he starts parading in uniform.

The Berserker: Driven to madness by all the vampire attacking and killing, this person takes on a psychotic existence, killing people he suspects of being vampires. He cannot be reasoned with, and trying to disarm him would be a lethal exercise. You have the right to defend yourself against this lunatic.

Freelancing Mercenaries: The ex-military contractors who handled various jobs for the Department of Defense when true military forces were unavailable might decide to form their own little army and carry out operations beyond any contractual duties they had. They might become very demanding in this way, taking over towns or setting up on private property with little heed for law or individual rights. Resist these wackos as best you can.

Indefinite Martial Law

A continued military and police presence for up to a year after the start of the uprising will probably be necessary in some places. The factors of the military occupation—mainly local and regional curfews and military enforcement of law—will continue as well. Three things will be necessary for a return to previous freedoms:

1. Return of all military forces to their bases and reassertion of civilian control of security at all levels of government (includes the conclusion of martial law in any state, as well as military- or mercenary-enforced roadblocks and curfews).
2. Congressional plan for economic recovery signed by the president, and return of at least half the working population to some kind of capital-generating employment.
3. Return of *habeas corpus* by presidential writ, as demanded by news and media organizations and many other citizens.

Don't expect all of these things to happen quickly or easily. Many Americans, for some strange reasons, don't seem to mind living in an authoritarian state as long as they're physically "safe." Generals and feds like power, because giant budgets and a lot of authority is what their professional lives are all about, and they have their doubts about "the Great Unwashed" anyway.

Food Shortages and Water Issues

While both the military and FEMA will have put forth a lot of effort to keep the tap running and the saturated fats in your belly, the periods of mercantile immobility are going to produce lingering shortages. Some wacky vampires will have tried to poison water sources, as a parting insult to a food source that fought back. But in most cases, treatment plants and reservoir systems will simply have been untended for long periods as workers protected their homes and

Random Question: Will there always be vampires in the United States of America?

Yes, there will be. There have been since before Europeans arrived, and there will continue to be so. And as much as the vampire uprising seems like a kind of historical outrage, there have been such waves of vampires in various countries and on various continents for centuries. In geological terms, this was a hundredth of a second, a quick fever. Humans and vampires will continue to evolve together.

families. Bringing everything back online will take time, especially at American ports, where material that couldn't be delivered for months will eventually start moving on trucks.

About a month to six weeks from the time that the military declares that major operations are ceasing, and a "mopping up" phase has begun, regular food distribution to supermarkets and mini-marts should begin to return to pre-uprising status. Restaurants will also return to nighttime service.

Any water treatment and sewage systems maintained by the army will transfer back to civilian control.

Civil Unrest

This will be a major factor affecting the return to pre-uprising liberties and civilian control. Numerous cities that experienced a lot of combat against vampires will see a sudden rise in crime as the vampires leave and any significant military or security presence decreases. A massive amount of looting and corruption will plague the return of a full-scale consumer economy; black marketers will attempt to control the distribution and sale of numerous goods as they try to grow their business into (semi-)legitimate operations. Breakdowns in relations that occurred during the vampire attacks will have consequences. Many Americans will have been in survival mode for a long time, and politeness is not a survival tactic, so there will be conflicts caused by incivility. Gang-related crime and violence surrounding the drug trade will increase in the months after the vampires recede as traffickers will once again have consumers that can move about freely, that have gone without actual meds for months, and are unbelievably stressed.

All Your Old Problems Come Back

At some point, the various parts of your old life will come into play, and previously unsolved problems will demand your attention. When the full-scale fighting is over, you'll have to start pulling your "normal" life back together, and that will include the usual load of irksome and seriously troubling details. And as much "celebration of America" as there will be in this period, with the president commissioning civilian Medals of Valor to be minted and awarded to regular folks who fought, most likely you're not going to get a ton of recognition for your battles against the bloodsuckers. Your family will—or should—thank you, and your

Vampire Fact:
A devil-vampire connection might have arisen out of the Vlad Dracula legends, given that his father's name, Dracul, means "devil" or "dragon" in old Romanian. In 1431, Vlad Dracul joined the Order of the Dragon, a Christian organization that dedicated itself to fighting the Turks. Members of the Order of the Dragon were supposed to wear the symbol of the order visibly, although both Vlad Dracul and Vlad Dracula had political dealings with the Turks.

neighbors and friends should, too, and that'll be about it.

There will also be a major new problem: employment. If your old job is waiting for you, post-uprising, you'll be lucky. Economic slowdown or, if you're willing to use the R-word, recession, will cause many businesses to temporarily lay off employees as the service economy begins to recover. This will have a major impact on mortgage payments, personal debt, savings and investments, and child-support payments. Bankruptcy claims, which climbed during the chaos, will skyrocket in this period.

Going Out After Dark

Do you or don't you? Some people will forever avoid going out at night after this period of intense vampiric threat. But many will see a return to American nightlife as an assertion of victory and will host numerous after-dark parties and dinners.

The real question is: How many vampires will continue to actively hunt and kill us?

Most estimates and studies say that with enough Americans fighting back and with all available military units sent a-hunting, upwards of 25 percent of all vampires will be killed. Using various models, some derived from predatory social insect and pack-mammal studies, the FBI has determined

that around 80 percent of the surviving vampire horde will be satisfied with the major dent they put in an irresistible food supply and slide back into a much more stealthy existence. The remaining 20 percent, or about 67,500 vampires, will continue a ravaging approach to their diet. That's a lot. So if you find out that you live in a vampire hot spot, you might not have any choice but to maintain a significant level of security for many months. But you will also have the right to demand military and police protection for such areas after the main portion of the anti-vamp fighting is over.

That vigorous 20 percent of the vampire population, encouraged by the success of the uprising, will most likely enjoy additional hours of hunting when North America goes into the short days of winter. You will, unfortunately, possibly be shooting vampires around Hanukkah, Christmas, Kwanzaa, and Boxing Day.

Put simply, going out at night is going to be a scary and sometimes dangerous prospect for some time. Basic safety procedures will have to be maintained: Travel in groups, travel armed if you wish or can, communicate with your network about where you're going and when, and call ahead to people expecting you.

And you might put Halloween on hold, at least the year the chaos subsides. No one will want to take kids out in the dark just yet. Anyone who dresses up like a freak, monster, or, dear God, a vampire, will risk death by gunshot. Americans being Americans, we'll probably throw some hellacious Halloween parties (even during the major uprisings), but if you're one of those people who like to run around the neighborhood and try to scare people with your O. J. Simpson mask, you might make out your will first.

Afterword

The nitty-gritty of survival tends to reshape a person's view on life. Not every adaptation that you develop will be likable, but knowing that you've got what it takes to make it through seriously bad times should give you a bit of confidence and frankness about what you might have to do in the future, in times of renewed vampire attack and other kinds of civil unrest.

But what now? Is this how it's going to be—random vampire attack on any given night? While a period of widespread, large-scale vampire uprising might not occur again for a number of years, individual vampires or small groups of bloodsuckers can occupy a region or county and quietly stay at work.

So, yes, this is how it's going to be for a while, because this is how history and the planet work.

You can think of it in Biblical terms, as if this has been a plague of very big, bad locusts, or think scientifically, as if this has been, literally, the spread of a virulent disease that will burn through its active phase and then be found in small occurrences for a number of years, only to arise again.

Once this uprising is quelled and there's a chance to take stock, all things vampire-related in America will soar: university studies, TV dramas, and numerous anti-vampire lotions, sprays, and nutritional supplements. Economic studies on the impact of the vampire uprising will occupy many bright minds. New lines of mood-affecting drugs will be introduced to treat vampire-related paranoia and depression due to blood loss. Entire research wings of the Christian, Judaic, and Islamic churches will be dedicated to anti-vampire study and efforts. Faith-based vampire-hunter teams will verge on vigilantism. The goths will have to form their own defense leagues.

Where does all that leave you? Most people will get back to the regular life that was so badly disrupted for those many months. But there will be a few Americans drawn to what

might be termed "vampire interdiction." If you earned a reputation in your neighborhood as a vampire killer, and you found your work and your adversary more than intriguing, perhaps you experienced something of a calling.

Start your own vampire-hunting business? Get a degree in vampire forensics? Become the foremost vampire artist-profiler, helping create highly detailed portraits of the most-wanted bloodsuckers for American intelligence services? There are a number of ways to go now that the threat of widespread vampirism has returned to North America.

Whatever you do, don't forget that life changes at sundown. Keep an eye out for the odd footprint in the yard, the scratch in the wood of the cellar door, the pallid face in the window at night . . .